Victoria Torres

Unfortunately Average

VICKA FOR PRESIDENT

by Julie Bowe

STONE ARCH BOOKS
a capstone imprint

All About Me

Hi, I'm Victoria Torres—Vicka for short. Not that I am short. Or tall. I'm right in the middle, otherwise known as "average height for my age." I'm almost twelve years old and just started sixth grade at Middleton Middle School. My older sister, Sofia, is an eighth grader. My little brother, Lucas, is in kindergarten, so that puts me in the middle of my family too:

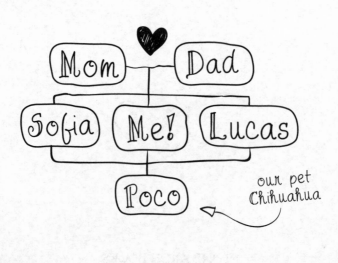

our pet Chihuahua

Victoria Torres, Unfortunately Average
is published by Stone Arch Books,
A Capstone Imprint
1710 Roe Crest Drive
North Mankato, Minnesota 56003
www.mycapstone.com

Cataloging-in-Publication Data is available on the Library of Congress website.

ISBN 978-1-4965-3800-0 (library binding)
ISBN 978-1-4965-3808-6 (paperback)
ISBN 978-1-4965-3814-7 (eBook PDF)

Summary: Middleton Middle School is holding class elections, and Victoria Torres decides
to throw her unfortunately-average hat in the ring. But when the campaign turns dirty,
Victoria can't help but wonder if shining as class president is even worth it.

Designer: Bobbie Nuytten
Image credits: Shutterstock: Brent Hofacker, 156, Kostsov, (badges), Cover,
Picsfive, (spray bottle), Cover, sakepaint, (pig), Cover
Illustrations: Sandra D'Antonio
Design elements: Shutterstock

Printed in China.
009581F16

I'm average in other ways too. I live in a middle-sized house at the center of an average town. I get Bs for grades, sit in the middle of the flute section in band, and can hit a baseball only as far as the shortstop. And even though she would say I'm "above average," I'm not always the BEST best friend to my BFF, Bea.

Still, my parents did name me Victoria—as in victory? They had high hopes for me right from the start! This ye determined to be average in ev

Chapter 1

The Race Is On

"I have some good news and some bad news," our history teacher, Mrs. Larson, announces in class on Monday afternoon.

"Tell us the good news first," my BFF, Bea, says. Bea is always looking on the bright side of things.

"The good news is that election season is upon us at Middleton Middle School," Mrs. Larson explains. "At the end of the month, each of you will have the opportunity to vote for your sixth-grade class officers! This is the perfect time to learn more about running for office. Therefore, I would like each of you to write a report about your favorite president!"

Everyone groans. "If writing a report is part of the *good* news," Henry says from a few desks behind me, "I'm afraid to hear what the *bad* news is!" He starts knocking his knees together and biting his nails like he's eating corn on the cob. We all laugh because Henry is such a clown.

"I have a hunch that learning more about your favorite president will inspire you to choose a great *class* president, so it *is* good news," Mrs. Larson replies. "Not to mention a great class treasurer and secretary too!"

"What about vice president?" asks my second-best friend, Jenny. "We need a V.P. too, don't we?"

"The office of vice president will go to the candidate who comes in second place in the presidential race," Mrs. Larson explains. "Historically, that's how the vice president was chosen in the early days of our national elections."

Annelise's hand shoots up in the air, making the bangles on her skinny arm rattle like a snake's tail.

"I have a very important announcement," she blares, waving her hand as she talks.

"Yes, Annelise?" our teacher asks. "What would you like to say?"

Annelise stands up and smooths down her new skirt. She was bragging to us about it before school. Her mom bought it for her this weekend. Unfortunately, Annelise brags to us most Monday mornings because she goes shopping almost every weekend. Her parents have lots of money to spend on her and her little brother because their dad is boss of an advertising agency and their mom is some kind of lawyer. My parents both work too, but we don't have tons of money to throw around.

Annelise clears her throat. "I would like to declare my candidacy for sixth-grade class president!"

The room goes dead silent. Henry starts to slow-clap. Some of his buddies snicker.

Quickly, Annelise gives Katie and Grace the eye. They are Annelise's best friends even though she usually treats them more like servants. Sometimes I think they just pretend to like her so she'll buy stuff for them when they go shopping together.

Katie and Grace take the hint and burst into applause. They get some of the other girls to join in until Annelise relaxes her glare and stands straight and tall, basking in the attention.

"Oh, brother," Henry mumbles.

"Oh, sister," Drew adds.

I sneak a glance behind me and see Drew and Henry cracking up. Sam is mimicking Annelise, pursing his lips and pretending to toss back his long, golden hair.

Fortunately, Drew doesn't see me watching him. If he did, my face would probably turn as red as a spicy pepper! Drew is the most popular boy in our class; I am the most average girl. It's silly for me to have a crush on him, but I do.

As soon as the applause dies away, Annelise says, "As all of you know, I would make a great class president. I'm super friendly and nice. I'm also very popular with everyone!" Bea and I look across the room at each other and roll our eyes.

"I already have lots of fantabulous ideas for turning this rat hole into a place we can finally be proud of. For example, who decided *mud brown* was a good color for these ugly desks? Not a girl, that's who. Only boys and pigs would want to sit at a mud-colored desk. With me as president, you can count on cool desk colors, like magenta and turquoise!"

Katie and Grace squeal. Their favorite colors are magenta, turquoise, and anything that doesn't clash with lime green.

"But mud brown is my favorite color," Henry says. "In fact, I *love* mud. I want to marry it." He puckers his lips and kisses his desk!

Everyone cracks up, except Annelise. "Like I said," she sasses, "only boys and *pigs* like mud."

Henry looks at her and snorts. "Oink, oink!" Then he blows a kiss at Annelise!

Her chin practically falls to the floor as the room explodes with laughter.

As soon as Mrs. Larson gets things under control again, Drew eagerly raises his hand. "We need more mud around this place," he says. "I nominate Henry for class president!"

Annelise gasps. "You can't do that!"

"In fact, he can," Mrs. Larson says. "Anyone may nominate a candidate for class president." She looks over at Henry. "So, Henry, what do you think? Do you accept Drew's nomination?"

Henry chuckles, waving her off. "Forget it, Mrs. L. The Drewster is just joking around."

But Drew doesn't back down. "I'm not joking, Hen," he says. "I nominate you for class president."

Henry shakes his head. "Then I'm inclined to decline the nomination!" he replies.

Drew leans in. "If you won't accept my nomination, then you leave me no choice. I *dare* you to run for president!"

The whole room gasps. No boy can turn down a dare! I think it's an oath they take at birth.

"*Oooh!*" Sam says, twitching like he just downed three cans of soda. "Didya hear that? Didya? Drew *dared* Henry to run for president!"

The air buzzes with excited whispering as we wait for Henry to make up his mind.

Sam and some of the other boys start pounding their mud-colored desks. "Hen-ry! Hen-ry! Hen-ry!" they chant.

Henry goes as pale as a beluga whale. He pushes back his sweaty bangs and turns to Mrs. Larson for backup.

But our teacher just smiles at Henry and says, "The decision is yours, Henry. Are you throwing your hat into the ring? That's actually an old boxing phrase, but presidential candidates have been using it for years."

Henry gulps like he just got punched in the stomach. "I . . . I . . . but . . ." The chanting grows louder.

Annelise growls and points a perfectly manicured finger at Henry. "If you *dare* to run against me, Henry Humphrey, you will regret it!"

Uh-oh! Bad idea, Annelise. Henry may hate the idea of running for president, but he loves to annoy Annelise. "Bring it on," he tells her. He turns to Drew. "I accept your dare . . . er . . . nomination."

Drew whoops.

Annelise scowls.

"Excellent!" Mrs. Larson exclaims. "We have a real race now! Anyone else care to step up and be counted?" She looks around the room. A few kids shrug. The rest of us shake our head no. Then Bea timidly raises her hand. "I don't want to be class president . . ." she blurts when Annelise whips a look at her, ". . . but I think I would make a good treasurer. I like math and I know my way around a calculator."

Lots of kids murmur in agreement, including me.

Grace fidgets in her chair for a moment, then raises her hand too. "I dunno, but I might want to be class secretary? I mean, I've got tons of gel pens. And I dot all my 'i's' with hearts and stuff."

Mrs. Larson smiles at Grace and Bea. "Wonderful!" she says. Then she looks around the room again, but no one else makes a peep. "Give it some thought," she says a moment later. "You have until noon tomorrow to sign up as a candidate in Principal Oates's office."

I raise my hand. "Mrs. Larson? You haven't told us what the bad news is yet."

"Oh!" she exclaims. "Thank you, Victoria, I almost forgot. I don't suppose it is *bad* news, exactly, but the fact remains that only one person can be elected to each office, even though many of you may be qualified for the job." Mrs. Larson smiles. "May the best candidate win!"

I glance at bossy Annelise, then further down the row at our class clown, Henry. Both of them want to be our new class president. But only *one* of them will win the election. I wonder which one it will be?

Chapter 2

A Crazy Idea

At supper later, I tell my family about our upcoming election for class officers and the dare that got Henry into the race. "Annelise is super upset that Henry is running against her."

Lucas looks up from his hot dog and mashed potatoes. He has a very worried look on his face. "You're not going to run for president, are you, Vicka? I don't want to move to the White House!"

Everyone chuckles. "Don't worry, Lucas," I tell my little brother. "I'm not running for office. Besides, we are electing a *class* president, not the president of our country. No one will have to move."

Lucas sighs with relief and sneaks a bite of his hot dog to Poco, who is begging for scraps. "Good!" he says. "I like living here!"

"What about you, Sofia?" Dad asks, shooing Poco away from the table. "Are you gunning to be an eighth-grade class officer?"

Sofia shakes her head. "I don't have time. I'm in charge of math club, plus I'm on student council this year." Her eyebrows furrow into a frown. "Wait a minute . . ." she says, looking at me. "Isn't anyone else from your class running for president?"

I shake my head. "Not that I know of. The deadline is tomorrow and so far only Annelise and Henry have thrown their hats into the ring. That's a boxing phrase, actually," I add smartly.

Sofia doesn't seem impressed by my boxing terminology. She just drops her hot dog, groans, and sinks back in her chair. "That's terrible news!"

"What's the matter, Sofie?" Lucas asks. "Don't you like boxing?"

"Yes," Sofia says. "I mean no. I mean, I'm not talking about boxing. I'm talking about Annelise and Henry running for president. *That's* what's terrible!"

"Why?" I ask. "You're not in sixth grade."

"Obvi," Sofia replies. "But the student council has to work with all the middle-school class officers to plan the big spring fund-raiser, later this year. If no one else runs for president of your class, *I'm* going to be stuck working with bossy Annelise and that goofball Henry! Just the other day, I saw him running someone's gym shorts up the school's flagpole. And the last time I was at the coffee shop in town, Annelise was there insisting that the barista redo her mocha because the chocolate sprinkles weren't evenly distributed across the top!"

Sofia gives me a pleading look. "There must be someone else in your class who would make a good president."

I think for a moment. "Bea is already running for class treasurer. And Jenny is too busy with sports and stuff." I think about Drew. He's definitely popular enough to get elected, but he's helping Henry win.

Dad wipes his mouth with a napkin. "I can think of someone in your class who would make a good president," he chimes in.

"Who?" I ask.

"You," he replies.

I open my eyes so wide my glasses slip down my nose! *"Me?!* That's crazy. I'm not running for president!"

But Sofia snaps at Dad's idea like it's a fishhook. "Why not?" she asks me. "You're always saying how you want to stand out in the crowd. What better way to get noticed than to be the president of your whole class?"

"But ... but ... but ..." I sputter, like a tugboat. "No one would vote for me. Most of the kids in my class don't even know who I am!"

"That's what campaigning is for," Mom says, siding with Dad. She always does. "You'll have plenty of time before Election Day to meet the voters and tell them about your plans for the future."

"Plans?!" I exclaim. "I don't have a plan, other than getting *murdered* by Annelise if I run against her! She'll get all the girls to vote for her anyway. And all the boys will vote for Henry. I'm not big and popular, like him. And I'm not pretty and pushy, like Annelise. I might as well be invisible! No one would vote for an average girl like me."

"That's not true," Mom says. "You are pretty *and* popular. Besides, presidents come in all shapes. For example, our nation's fourth president, James Madison, wasn't much taller than you are. He weighed less than a hundred pounds! Abraham Lincoln was tall and gawky. As a child, some people thought he was lazy because all he wanted to do was read books and write poetry, rather than help with the chores. Madison and Lincoln didn't fit the mold of a future president, but they believed in making a difference and gained the voters' confidence along the way."

I push mashed potatoes around on my plate, thinking about Mom's little speech. I *do* care about making a difference at my school. And, like Sofia said, being president of my class would really make me shine this year. But getting kids to vote for plain old me is an unfortunately huge problem! And believing I could actually get elected is the biggest problem of all.

I glance over the top of my glasses at my sister. "If I *did* run for president, which I am *not* . . . what would I have to do?"

Sofia slides her plate aside and leans in. "Make posters. Schmooze with your classmates. Tell them who you are and how you will change the school. Act friendly, be confident, and give a great speech to all your classmates."

My eyes go buggy again. "But I'm terrible at giving speeches! I always lose my place and blank out, or mumble so fast no one can understand what I'm saying."

"That's what I'm here for," Sofia says reassuringly. "As your campaign manager, you'll win this election *if it's the last thing I do.*"

I gulp like I just swallowed my hot dog sideways. Sofia can be really tough to deal with when she sets her mind on something. I look around the table at my family. Mom and Dad are giving me "Go for it!" smiles. Sofia is already tossing around campaign slogans. Lucas is bouncing up and down on his chair, chanting like a cheerleader. "Vote! For! Vicka! Vote! For! Vicka!" Even my pooch, Poco, is scampering around the table, yipping and wagging his tail like someone just promised him a whole platter of hot dogs.

"It's up to you, Vicka," Dad says as he and Mom begin to clear away the dishes. "We won't force you to run, but it could be a real confidence booster for you!"

Mom nods. "And, win or lose, it would help you meet lots of your classmates and find out what interests them. I think you'd make a great president,

Victoria Torres! You are smart, kind, and likable. Who could resist voting for you?"

I sink back in my chair, feeling as wimpy as a soggy mud puddle. My whole family thinks I should run for president, but all I want to do is run away!

Chapter 3

PEE-YOO!

The next morning, I quickly slurp down a bowl of cereal for breakfast, then zip out the door before anyone in my family has a chance to pester me again about running for president. Because I have decided that, if I did, it would be a supersized disaster, with a side order of misery. I can barely lead Poco to the park without getting his leash tangled around a light post. And when I'm in charge of Lucas, he usually spills something on the carpet, or locks himself in a cupboard, or drops an action figure down the toilet. Leading my entire class through the whole school year? No way.

Jenny meets up with Bea and me before school. "Cute haircut!" I tell Jenny. Her hair used to be long like mine, but now it's cut in layers that just skim her shoulders.

"Thanks!" Jenny replies. "I wanted it shorter for volleyball, so I got it cut at the mall after practice yesterday. But that's not all I got." Jenny unclips a little bottle of body spritz from her backpack. "I ran into Annelise at the beauty boutique that's next to the hair place. She had just bought a gazillion spritzes, all different scents. Mine is green apple. Try some!"

Jenny spritzes Bea and me. I sniff my sleeve. "It smells apple-icious!" I say. "But why was Annelise buying so many? And, no offense, but why did she give one to you? Usually she only buys stuff for her popular friends, not us."

"She's giving spritzes to everyone in our whole class. It's part of her PEE-YOO! campaign. She told me all about it at the mall."

"Her *what*?" Bea and I ask at the same time.

"P-E-E-Y-O-O," Jenny explains. "It stands for *Proclamation Ending EverY Offensive Odor.* As president, Annelise plans to make our school a stink-free zone. Handing out body spritz is just the start. She also wants to put air fresheners in all the lockers and deodorant in every gym bag . . . *especially* in all of the the boys' lockers and gym bags."

Bea jiggles excitedly. *"Oooh* . . . I can't wait until Annelise gets here! I hope she got honeysuckle spritz. That's my favorite!"

"You're planning to vote for Annelise?" I ask, surprised. "I thought for sure you'd vote for Henry." Even though Bea won't admit it, I think she has a secret crush on him.

Bea shakes her head. "I'm not going to vote for Annelise, I just want some spritz. If she asks me to vote for her, I'll just tell her I might."

I gasp. Bea is the most honest person I know. The only time she ever fibs is when she sneaks perfume and hair mousse from her older sister's room and then denies it when Jazmin catches her smelling like a flirty gummy worm. "But that's lying!"

"No it's not," Bea replies matter-of-factly. "It's politics. I can say that I'm voting for one candidate and then, on Election Day, I can choose someone else. Each person's vote is secret. No one can tell me who to pick."

Jenny nods. "Annelise asked me to vote for her when she gave me my spritzer. I said I'd think about it." She shrugs. "I have, and I think it would be a terrible idea!"

Bea giggles and gives Jenny a high five. Then she turns to me. "Don't look so shocked, Vicka. You know everything is a popularity contest with Annelise. The only way she can get people to like her is by buying their votes. If she runs out of spritz, her parents will just buy her more."

I can't disagree with Bea about that. "But to me, it seems like the most important thing about running for president is getting everyone to like your *ideas*, not just getting them to like the stuff you buy for them."

Jenny nods thoughtfully. "Good point, Vicka. You should run for president! I would totally vote for you!"

"*¡Uf!*" I say. "Now you sound like my family. They were trying to convince me to throw my hat into the ring last night."

Bea brightens. "Do it, Vicka! Run for class president! Then we won't have to vote for snarky Annelise *or* goofy Henry!" She leans in to whisper. "But don't tell Henry I said that. And please don't announce your candidacy until *after* I get my honeysuckle spritz, okay?"

I roll my eyes at Bea. "No worries, because I'm not going to run for office. I'm the last person anyone would vote for! Henry is super funny and popular with all the boys. Annelise can afford to buy cool swag for all the girls. I'm not popular or rich. I'm only me, Victoria Torres, unfortunately average. Far from presidential material."

"But you just said being prez shouldn't be about popularity," Jenny corrects me. "It should be about making a difference at our school."

Bea agrees. "You may be average, but you have something Henry and Annelise don't have."

I give Bea a puzzled look. "What?"

"Us!" Bea says, linking elbows with Jenny. "We'll help you win the election!"

"Vicka for president!" Jenny shouts.

Bea shushes her. "Keep it low, Jen . . . remember? I haven't gotten my spritz yet!"

The more we giggle together, the more I warm up to the idea of running for president. With friends like these by my side, how can I lose?

Chapter 4

Smells Like Trouble

By the time lunch hour rolls around, Bea smells like a honeysuckle forest. Jenny smells like a ginormous box of sour apple jawbreakers. Both of them have me convinced that running for president would totally make me shine.

We eat lunch fast, then we head to Principal Oates's office so I can add my name to the list of candidates. Bea signed up as a candidate for treasurer yesterday. Every clump of girls we pass along the way smells like a bowl of jelly beans—strawberry, cherry, banana, tangerine!—I hate to admit it, but Annelise already has our school smelling good.

So far I've managed to avoid Annelise all day. I'm not looking forward to her finding out I'm running for class prez too. She told Henry he would regret it if he ran against her. What will Annelise do when she finds out I'm running against her too?

Unfortunately, I'm about to find out. As Bea, Jenny, and I round the corner to Principal Oates's office, there's Annelise, handing out spritzers with Katie and Grace. A couple of other girls from our class—Felicia and Julia—are helping too.

"Don't be a stinker! Vote for Annelise!" they shout, spritzing kids as they walk by. They even surround Drew, Henry, and Sam, spritzing them as they duck and dodge the fruity spray.

"Give me *mud* or give me death!" Henry shouts as Drew tries to protect his candidate from the spray.

Jenny nudges me with her elbow. "You're going to need a fantabulous plan to keep up with Annelise and Henry. Look at all the girls, chasing down the boys for her. And the guys are ready to go to battle for Henry!"

"But I don't have a plan at all," I say, feeling my confidence fizzle. "And the only people I've got on my side are you and Bea. I better back out now before—"

Bea grabs my arm and tugs me toward the office. "Think positive," she says encouragingly.

"Okay," I mumble, dragging my feet. "I'm *positive* this is a bad idea."

When Annelise sees Bea, Jenny, and me coming toward her, she smiles so big I can practically see what she ate for lunch. "Thanks for coming to support me!" she says, running up to us. "I'm going to need every girl's vote in order to beat Henry and the boys."

Annelise holds open the shopping bag she's carrying so we can look inside. "Help yourself to a spritzer," she says. "I have tons more in my locker. Daddy is getting the cutest blingy buttons and sparkly T-shirts made too! I'll bring them tomorrow. All the girls will want one."

Bea and Jenny dig through the bag of body sprays as Annelise explains her PEE-YOO! project to us.

"Daddy helped me think of it. He's got tons of clever ideas to make me a winner. Go on, Vicka, what are you waiting for? Take a spritzer!"

"Score!" Bea says, pulling a minibottle from the bag. "I got honeysuckle again!"

Annelise smiles, pleased. "Take as many as you want. Stick with me, and you'll never stink again!" She nudges the bag toward me.

"Um . . ." I say as Bea and Jenny start a spritz war with Katie, Grace, Felicia, and Julia while the guys take cover in the boys' restroom. "Thanks, but I don't think I should take one."

"Why not?" Annelise asks, surprised. "Don't tell me you're allergic or something."

"No," I reply. "But you bought the spritzers for kids who plan to vote for you. And . . . the thing is . . . I'm planning to vote for someone else."

Annelise practically drops the bag. "Why would you want to vote for a doofus like Henry? He smells worse than a gym sock! I don't think he owns a comb, much less shampoo. The only thing he's good at is telling jokes."

I take a deep breath. "I'm not voting for Henry. Or you. I've decided to run for class president too."

Now Annelise's eyes go as wide as her hoop earrings.

"*You?* Why? You can't win. And you'll take votes away from *me*. Then Henry will win for sure, and we'll be stuck with a clown for a president!"

I fidget, not knowing what to say. Annelise is right. Henry is only in this race because Drew dared him to run. He doesn't want to lead our class in anything other than goofing around and having fun. Soon Annelise and her friends will shine with blingy buttons and sparkly T-shirts. All the glitter in the world couldn't make me shine as brightly as her.

Annelise tilts her hips. "Admit it, Vicka, I'm the *best* candidate for the job. Drop out now, before it's too late. With all the girls on my side, we can beat the boys for sure."

I frown. "But this shouldn't be about boys versus girls. It should be about electing a president who will work hard to make real changes at our school. With Bea and Jenny's help, I think I can do that."

"Do *what*?" Annelise persists. "Do you even have a plan?"

I bite my lip. "I'll have one. Soon. Probably."

Annelise shakes her head and *tsks* her tongue. Then she turns on her sparkly heel and marches over to Bea and Jenny. A moment later, she snatches their spritzers away.

"Hey!" Jenny shouts.

"That's mine!" Bea adds.

"Sorry," Annelise says in a not-sorry voice. "The spritzers are for my *friends*, not my *enemies*."

Annelise turns and glares at me. Then she herds the other girls away in a cloud of perfume.

I gulp. Annelise has a reputation for getting even with her enemies. Something tells me I'm going to have to watch my back from now until Election Day.

"Well, isn't this a pleasant surprise!" Principal Oates smiles at Bea, Jenny, and me as she returns from lunch and unlocks her office door. "I'm not usually so popular."

"We're here to sign up for the election," Jenny explains. "Bea already signed up for class treasurer. Now Vicka wants to be president!"

Principal Oates smiles at Bea and me. "I saw Bea's name on the list this morning! Step inside and we'll sign you up too, Victoria!"

I try to smile as I add my name to the list of sixth-grade candidates. But it's hard to feel happy when you are fearing for your life.

Fortunately, Annelise is nowhere in sight when we head out into the hallway again.

*Un*fortunately, Drew is still hanging around. As usual, I morph into a complete stone-faced statue as soon as he walks up to us. "Whoa, Vicka," he says with surprise. "Don't tell me you got in trouble with the principal!"

"She's not in trouble," Bea explains when she sees I've gone stone-faced. "None of us are. We were just signing up for the election. I'm running for treasurer and Vicka is running for president!"

Drew looks at us, impressed. "I'll vote for you, Bea. I'd vote for you too, Vicka, if Henry wasn't in the race. I've gotta have his back though, you know?"

I manage to nod.

Drew grins, then gives Jenny and Bea a high five. "TTYL!" he shouts, then takes off down the hall, practically tripping over Annelise, who is watching from around the corner.

Annelise crosses her arms and smirks at me. "What's the matter, Vicka?" she asks, glancing from me to Drew as he disappears out of sight. "Did your *crush* take your breath away?"

"He . . . he's not my crush," I stutter.

"Uh-huh. Sure. Right." Annelise's lips curl into a Grinch-sized smile. "Don't worry," she singsongs. "Your secret is safe with me."

Chapter 5

Stumped!

I stop by the library after school to pick up some books about presidents for my research paper. I still don't know which president I want to write about, so I check out a bunch of stuff. The library is near my family's music store, The Middle Si, so I lug my stack there afterward and catch a ride home with Dad.

"I didn't get a chance to talk with you this morning before school," Dad says as we drive. "What did you decide about running for class president?"

"We had to sign up yesterday," I tell him. "I almost chickened out, but in the end, I added my name to the list of candidates."

"Bravo, Bonita!" Dad exclaims, calling me by his pet name for me. It means *pretty little one* in Spanish. "I'm proud of you for being brave. You will learn a lot during the campaign. And I know you will make *un excelente presidente!*"

I sigh. "Thanks, but I can't be an excellent president, or even an average one, if I don't have a platform. Mrs. Larson taught us that term in history class. It means having a plan for what you'll do if you're elected. Annelise plans to make our school less smelly. She wants to put air fresheners in every locker and make the boys wear deodorant after P.E."

Dad chuckles. "Good luck with that."

"Henry doesn't really have a plan," I continue, "but no one seems to care. He's all about joking around and having fun. I like having fun too, and I'd rather smell like a pack of gum than a sweat sock, but it seems like there must be something more important for a class president to stand for than smelling good and getting lots of laughs."

Dad turns into our driveway and pulls to a stop by the garage. "It sounds to me like you need a plan that is somewhere in the middle—part fun and part popular."

"*¡Uf!*" I say, letting my head fall back against the seat. "I'm trying to get out of the middle, Dad! I want to be president so I can shine!"

Dad smiles. "And you will," he says. "Just think about the things that spark your interest. What issues get you really excited? Which ones make your blood boil? That's the mark of a true leader—someone who is passionate about the things that matter most.

"Choose an issue that's important to you and your school, not just the one that will get you elected. Then others will sense your enthusiasm and want to be part of it. If you give your classmates an issue to chew on, they'll have to think about what really matters to them too. That's the best way to shine, Vicka. Do that and, win or lose, you will have made a difference at your school."

I think about Dad's advice all week. What excites and challenges me? What do I feel passionate about? How can I spark my classmates' interest too?

Unfortunately, I don't come up with any spectacular answers. That's because average girls like me spend most of their time worrying about average things, like getting Bs instead of Cs on my quizzes and trying not to trip when I'm carrying my food through the lunchroom.

Earlier this year I *did* trip and almost landed in the big trash can where everyone dumps their lunch leftovers. Fortunately, Bea caught me before I went face first into a mountain of apple cores, banana peels, napkins, and milk cartons. *Un*fortunately, Drew happened to be standing right there. My messy tray landed—*splat!*—upside-down on his brand new running shoes!

As I slip into my desk for history class on Friday afternoon, I still haven't come up with a platform for my campaign. Maybe Mrs. Larson will teach us something today that will give me a bright idea. I take out my sparkliest pencil, sharpen it to a perfect point, then open my history notebook to a crisp, new page and get ready for the perfect idea to blink across my brain like a theater marquee.

"Today, I want to spend our class time learning about stump speeches," Mrs. Larson says as everyone takes their seats.

"*Stump* speeches?" Sam scratches his head. "Is that what George Washington gave after he cut down his dad's cherry tree?"

"Hey, yeah," Henry chimes in. "I know that story. The dude was just a kid when he did it. Afterward, he fessed up to his old man, and they've been calling him Honest Abe ever since." Everyone laughs at how Henry has jokingly combined the stories of two of our best known presidents.

"Actually, the story of Washington and the cherry tree is a legend," Mrs. Larson says. "Which means it's probably not true. And the nickname, Honest Abe, refers to our sixteenth president, Abraham Lincoln, although George Washington was admired for his honesty too."

"Oh," Henry says. "My bad. So what's a stump speech then?"

"*Stump speech* is a term that came into use years after Washington's presidency," Mrs. Larson explains. "Back then, candidates traveled across the frontier, delivering the same speech over and over again to small groups of townspeople and farmers. They often stood on a sawed-off tree stump to address their audiences, telling about their plans for the future and discussing the issues that concerned them. Even though politicians stand on stages to deliver their speeches today, the term *stump speech* is still used."

Mrs. Larson pauses, looking around the room at all of us. "Today I'm challenging each of you to think about one specific issue that concerns you. Then I'd like you to prepare a six-word stump speech about it."

Drew raises his hand. "Did you mean to say a six-*minute* speech, Mrs. Larson?"

Our teacher shakes her head. "You heard me correctly, Drew. You'll each have five minutes to prepare a speech that must be exactly six words long. It could address a big issue, like overpopulation or global warming. Or it could cover something smaller and closer to home, like picking up litter around town, or . . ." she pauses to give Henry a sly glance. ". . . or making our school a bit muddier."

Everyone snickers. Henry beams.

"But I need at least six *hundred* words to tell everyone about my PEE-YOO! project!" Annelise complains.

"Six words," Mrs. Larson repeats firmly. "No more, no less. That's part of the challenge of this assignment." She checks her watch. "You have five minutes, starting . . . now."

Annelise frowns. But she grabs a piece of paper and a pencil and gets to work.

We all do.

Some kids start jotting down ideas right away. Other kids, like me, doodle on the edges of our notebooks, trying to think of an issue we are passionate about. I care about lots of things—dolphins, for example. And being an astronaut someday, so I can discover life on other planets.

But I want to pick a smaller issue that's close to home, like Mrs. Larson suggested. Plus, I want the issue to be something everyone will like because it's fun. I think a little longer, then write, *We can have fun making a difference together* on my paper. I count the words.

Eight.

That's too many words, so I start crossing some out and juggling others around.

Work together, have fun, make a difference.

Seven words this time. I'm getting closer! But it's still not a speech about an issue.

"Time's up!" Mrs. Larson says. "Pencils down."

¡Uf! My stump speech is too long and it's too general. Unfortunately, there's nothing I can do about that now.

We start going around the room, sharing our speeches.

"Save all the trees, pretty please."

"Peace is good. War is bad."

"Exploring space is far out, dude."

"Global warming is not very cool."

"You smell bad, I don't. Ha."

"Don't forget to reduce, reuse, recycle."

"Mud! Mud! Mud! Mud! Mud! Mud!"

Some of the stump speeches are silly, like Henry's mud one, but most of them remind me of issues I care about. Felicia's makes me think of the recycling bins my parents set up on our porch so we can sort our glass, plastic, and metal containers. Sam's speech reminds me of how much I love space stuff too, and that exploring other galaxies teaches us a lot about our own.

"Vicka?" Mrs. Larson calls on me. "Care to share your stump speech with the class?"

I fiddle with the edge of my paper. "Okay, but it's not done yet."

"A work in progress," Mrs. Larson says. "Let's hear what you've got so far."

I clear my throat. "Work together, have fun, make a difference."

"That was *seven* words," Annelise snarks. "*My* speech was *six* words, on the dot."

"Vicka could change it up a little." Drew's voice trails up from the back of the room. "Maybe something like, 'Fun, working together, makes a difference.'" He looks at Annelise. "That was six words, on the dot."

Annelise makes a face at Drew.

"Hey, thanks, Drew," I say, rewriting my speech. "I like it."

Annelise snorts a laugh. "Of course you do. You'd like anything *Drew* says."

I freeze as giggles ripple across the room. I want to whip around and tell Annelise to shut her big, blabbing mouth. Instead, I close my eyes and take a deep breath, remembering something Mom told me the last time Annelise was being more annoying than usual: *Don't give a bully the satisfaction of a reaction.*

Mrs. Larson turns to the whiteboard, ignoring Annelise too, and soon the giggles fade away. She writes my six-word speech on the board. "I was just noticing that Vicka's speech works as a class motto. Regardless of who wins the election, working together as a class is key to making our school the best that it can be. And having fun while we do it isn't a bad idea either!"

Now whispers of agreement take a trip around the room. I smile. Mrs. Larson turned my speech into a motto! Now if I can only turn one idea into a platform, I will have something to catch the attention of my classmates.

"Two reminders before the bell rings for the last time this week," Mrs. Larson says as we begin to put our things away. "First, as part of our class elections, each of our presidential candidates will present a stump speech next week. In keeping with the tradition of traveling across the wild frontier, our candidates will travel across the wild lunchroom. And since we are fresh out of stumps at Middleton Middle School, our candidates will deliver their speeches from the top of a milk crate."

Annelise's hand shoots into the air. "I've already written *my* speech, Mrs. Larson," she says. "It's six *pages* long. I plan to memorize it."

"I plan to miss it," Drew mumbles under his breath.

I can't help but snicker.

"What's the second reminder, Mrs. Larson?" Henry asks.

"Don't forget to keep working on your president reports," Mrs. Larson says. "They're due the day before Election Day."

"Can the reports be six words long?" Henry asks, hopefully.

"Six *hundred* words should do it," Mrs. Larson replies.

Henry slumps. "I'm sorry I asked."

Chapter 6

Chew On This

"Rise and shine, Vicka," Sofia says, shaking my sleepy shoulders on Saturday. "We've got work to do."

"But it's the weekend," I mumble in my froggy morning voice. I roll over and squint at the clock on my nightstand. "*¡Ay,* Sofia! It's only 8:00! I sleep until at least 9:00 on Saturdays. Come back in an hour."

I roll away and pull the covers over my head.

Sofia yanks the blankets off me. "We have an election to win, Victoria Torres," she says.

I prop myself up on my elbows and frown at Sofia. "Why do you care so much about me winning the presidency, anyway? You're not in sixth grade."

"I already told you," Sofia replies, pulling a T-shirt and sweatpants from my dresser and tossing them at me. "I have to work with the new president on the spring fund-raiser. Besides, it would be an embarrassment if my little sister lost, now that she's declared her candidacy. We have my reputation to think about."

I groan. Sofia is super smart. All my teachers say so. She's even leading the middle school math club this year. But just between you and me, she can also be super bossy, like Annelise. No matter how much I argue with her, she always wins in the end.

"Fine," I say, waving my T-shirt like a white flag. "What do we have to do to win the election?"

Sofia stands before me and punches her fists into her hips. "Don't you ever listen to anything I say?!" she says.

"What?" I ask, rubbing the sleep from my eyes.

Sofia gives me a sassy squint. Then she starts counting off on her fingers. "Like I told you the other night, we have to print campaign posters, make buttons, write a speech, and build a platform."

"But we don't need to build a platform," I interrupt, yawning. "Mrs. Larson said we'll stand on a milk crate to give our stump speeches."

Now Sofia groans. "*Platform* as in a *plan,* not a stage. You'll have to tempt your classmates with a promise to get them to vote for you."

"Oh, *that* kind of platform," I say, putting on my glasses. "Annelise plans to make the school less stinky. Henry plans to make it more muddy."

"Lame and lamer," Sofia replies.

I shrug. "So far, all the girls like Annelise's plan, and all the boys like Henry's. I guess sixth graders like lame things."

"Unfortunately, you're right," Sofia says. "That makes you the underdog in this race."

"Woof," I say, falling back onto my bed.

Sofia pulls me up again. "Underdogs have to work harder than everyone else. Get dressed, Fido. Meet me at campaign headquarters in five minutes, and be ready to get to work."

"Where's campaign headquarters?" I ask, tugging on a pair of sweats.

"The dining room," Sofia replies. "We're taking it over until Election Day."

I grab a crumpled hoodie from the end of my bed and pull it on over my nightshirt. Then I look at myself in the mirror that hangs on the back of my bedroom door as Sofia heads downstairs. Major bed head. Smudgy glasses. Mismatched clothes. "I could be the poster child for underdogs," I say, turning to look at myself from all sides. "How will I ever beat someone as flashy as Annelise or as popular as Henry?"

I trudge downstairs, hoping Sofia will have the answer.

When I get to the dining room a minute later, Sofia is typing on her laptop. Lucas is munching dry cereal from the box and coloring on a big sheet of poster board. Mom's scrapbooking supplies are scattered across the table—colorful paper, washi tape, markers, glitter glue, stickers, and even a button-making machine.

"Look, Vicka!" Lucas cries as I walk into the room. He holds up the poster he's coloring. It's dotted with red, white, and blue stars. Across the top he's written, *To Vika, Frum Lucas.* "I'm helping you win your *champagne!*"

Sofia barks a laugh. "*Campaign*, Lucas, not champagne," she says, correcting our little brother.

Lucas picks up a brown crayon and goes back to work. "I'm drawing dogs on the poster too, Vicka, because Sofie says you are the underdog and need all the help you can get."

I give my sister a squint. "Gee, thanks."

Sofia shrugs. "The truth hurts."

Lucas looks up again, his eyes bright with an idea. "You should ask Poco to help too, Vicka! He knows all about being a dog!"

Poco perks up from where he was snoozing by Sofia's feet. He hops up and wags his tiny tail as I nab a piece of dry cereal from the box and hold it a few inches above his pink eraser nose.

"*¡Sientate*, Poco!" I say in a commanding voice.

Poco sits up on his hind legs and begs for the treat.

"Good dog!" I praise him and then toss the treat in the air. *Chomp!*

I grab another cereal nugget and twirl it around. "*¡Vueltas!*" I tell my pooch.

Poco rolls onto his back, then hops up and starts begging again.

I give him another treat. *Chomp-chomp!*

Picking up Poco, I hug his frisky little body. My dog is so smart, he even knows two languages!

"Check it out, Vicka," Sofia says, pushing back from her computer. "I thought we could use this design on some of your posters and buttons."

I set down Poco and look over Sofia's shoulder at the image on her screen.

"That design is übercool!" I tell my sister. "It looks so professional, like the posters Annelise hung around school the other day. Her dad made them at his advertising agency. He's making buttons and T-shirts for her too. And I heard Katie and Grace talking about the candy bars they'll be handing out at school on

Monday. Each one will have a sticker of Annelise on the wrapper." I laugh to myself. "Everyone is going to love ripping her picture in half to get at the chocolate."

"Maybe so, but giving away all that free stuff is getting lots of people to notice her," Sofia says in her practical way. "Still, it's not Annelise I'm worried about. Everyone knows she's a bossy brat. They're acting like they support her now so she'll keep giving them cool stuff, but that doesn't mean they will vote for her. When it comes to winning the most votes, Henry is the one we have to watch out for."

"Henry?!" I exclaim. "But he doesn't even care about winning. He's only running for president because Drew dared him to."

"That's just it," Sofia says. "The less he cares, the more people want to see if he can pull it off and win. They might vote for him, just to be in on the joke."

Unfortunately, my sister is probably right. Sixth graders definitely like to joke around. And Henry is the top joker in our class. "All Henry has to do is shout, 'Mud!' and everyone within earshot claps and cheers," I tell my sister.

Sofia nods. "Popularity rules."

I slump into a chair feeling as unpopular as a bag of brussels sprouts. Mom comes in from the kitchen with a bowl of fresh fruit for us to snack on. She sets the bowl on the table and says, "I have to work at the music store this morning, then get groceries on the way home. Abuela is stopping by to watch Lucas so you girls can keep working on Vicka's campaign. How's it coming along?"

"Good!" Lucas says cheerfully, drawing more dogs on the poster he's making.

"Bad," Sofia grumbles as she hunches over her computer.

I sigh and reach for a strawberry from the fruit bowl. "Thanks for your vote of confidence, Sofia."

"It's my job to tell it like it is," Sofia replies matter-of-factly. "The cutest posters in the world can't beat a popular platform."

Mom studies me for a moment. "By the look on your face, Victoria, I'd say you agree with your sister."

I shrug and nibble the strawberry. "Henry is funny and popular. Annelise is rich and glammy. I'm just plain and average. Unfortunately."

Mom smiles and sits down next to me. "Funny jokes and glittery promises only go so far. Your classmates will want substance too."

"Substance?" I make a face. "That sounds like the steel-cut oats you're always trying to get us to eat for breakfast."

"Substance has to do with an organized campaign," Mom continues, ignoring my oatmeal comment. "First, you need to show the voters you've got people backing you up. Apart from Sofia, who is helping with your campaign?"

"Bea and Jenny," I tell Mom.

"And me!" Lucas chimes in.

"And Lucas," I add.

Poco yips and wags his tail.

"Poco too," I say, tossing him another nugget of cereal.

"Great!" Mom says. "Next, you have to make the voters like you."

"*Ooh*!" Lucas says. "I know how to do that, Vicka! Buy everyone a video game! Then they will *love* you! Can you buy me one too?"

"I can't afford to buy video games for my whole class, Lucas," I say. "I'm not Annelise."

"What's something else everyone in your class likes?" Mom asks.

"I know what *my* class likes," Lucas chimes in.

"What?" I ask, even though he will probably say something silly, like Duck, Duck, Goose.

"Snacks!" Lucas cries. Then he takes a banana from the fruit bowl and grunts like a monkey.

I give my little brother a smile. "My class likes snacks too. But Annelise has already promised to bring candy bars for everyone on Monday. I can't hand out candy too or she'll call me a copycat."

"How about a healthy snack instead?" Mom suggests. She looks at the fruit bowl. "Apples . . . or strawberries? In fact, eating healthy could be part of your campaign platform."

I straighten up a little. "Dad did tell me to give my classmates an issue to *chew* on . . ." I say, thinking about healthy food and how everyone in my class—girls and boys—loves to eat snacks.

"Ugh, Vicka," Sofia says. "We want you to *win* the election. No kid is going to vote for a candidate who brings them apples for a snack and then promises to give them carrots and broccoli for lunch!"

But I'm still thinking while Sofia is busy complaining. "They might not mind the healthy food so much if we grew it ourselves."

Sofia shakes her head like I've lost my marbles, but I keep brainstorming. "If we grew a garden with veggies and berries and maybe even an apple tree, everyone could help take care of it, and we'd be making a big difference at our school!"

Now Sofia starts typing again, but Mom perks up. "You could even compost food scraps from the cafeteria," she offers. "Then there would be less waste in the lunchroom and more dirt to use in your garden."

"Dirt!" Lucas shouts, pumping his fist in the air. "The boys will like that idea, Vicka! I should know. I've been a boy my whole life."

We all laugh at Lucas's comment, but he's right. The boys would totally go for spending part of the school day outside, messing around in the dirt. And the girls would like it too. If my platform includes growing a school garden and composting food scraps, other grades could get involved too. We could have lots of gardens. Then I would really shine as president!

"I suppose Principal Oates would like the idea of a garden," Sofia says, warming up to my idea. "And there's a sunny corner in our school's courtyard that no one ever uses."

"Julia's parents own the greenhouse in town," I add. "She's in my class. Maybe they would donate some plants. And the lunch ladies are always pestering us about wasting food. They would probably love it if we compost our scraps instead of throwing them out with the trash."

I take a big bite of the sweet, juicy strawberry in my hand. Suddenly an above-average idea pops into my head. "Mom, could you buy a bunch of strawberries when you go to the grocery store, *por favor*?" I ask politely. "Enough for my whole class? Chocolate chips too, please? I'll help pay for everything with my allowance. Oh, and can I invite Bea and Jenny to a sleepover tonight? I need their help with something."

Mom raises her eyebrows curiously. "*Sí*," she replies. "But what are you cooking up, Victoria Torres?"

I smile, mysteriously. "I'm going to give my classmates something sweet *and* healthy to chew on!"

Chapter 7

Berry Good Friends

Later that evening, Jenny and Bea help me wash the big box of strawberries Mom bought at the grocery store today. The microwave beeps. I take out a glass bowl filled with melting chocolate chips and begin to stir the ooey-gooey sauce.

"*Mmm* . . ." Jenny says, patting the strawberries dry with a kitchen towel. "That chocolate sauce smells like heaven! Everyone will love eating straw-berries dipped in chocolate!"

"And don't forget about the sprinkles," Bea adds. She opens up shakers of red, white, and blue sprin-kles so we can make our strawberries really shine.

"They'll taste good *and* look great. These treats are going to rock our school, Vicka!"

Jenny, Bea, and I giggle together. Poco dances around my feet, yipping happily as we dip the berries in chocolate and sprinkle them with colorful sugar. He sits up and begs for a treat, even though chocolate is a no-no for dogs.

I ditch the berries for a moment and find a box of doggie treats instead. I twirl the treat above Poco. He dances in a circle on his stubby hind legs.

Bea looks over as Poco crunches his reward and dances for more. "If Poco were running for president, he would win in a landslide. No one could resist voting for such a cute puppy!"

"We can't let all that cuteness go to waste," Jenny adds. "Got a camera handy, Vicka? Let's do a doggie photo shoot! We can print posters and hang them around school!"

"I've got the perfect slogan," Bea says, dipping a strawberry into the bowl of warm chocolate sauce.

"What is it?" I ask, washing my hands and then coming back to help with the berries.

"Don't make me beg. Vote for Victoria!"

I tuck my paws under my chin and howl with happiness. "I love that slogan so much I want to *marry* it," I joke in a voice that sounds like Henry's.

Jenny bulks up her shoulders and shakes her bangs into her eyes, so she looks more like Henry. "Your slogan is the *berry* best, Bea," she says in a gruff voice. "And I'm not just sayin' that 'cause I like you."

Bea giggles like crazy. "Stop teasing, Jen! Let's hurry up and finish with the strawberries, so we can make the puppy posters!"

"You're running for class treasurer," Jenny says. "We could make treats and posters for you too, Bea!"

"Hey, that's a great idea!" I say, happy to help my best friend with her campaign too.

Bea giggles again as she starts to set the finished berries in the containers we'll use to bring them to school on Monday. "I don't have to go all out with treats and posters because no one is running against me! It would be fun to make a few posters, though. I have another good idea for a slogan."

"What is it?" I ask.

"You can *count* on me for treasurer!" She smiles at Jenny and me. "Get it? You can *count* on me?"

"We get it!" Jenny and I say together.

"Let's draw pictures of dollar bills on the posters," Jenny suggests. "Then we can stick Bea's photo in the middle, instead of ol' George."

"That would be really funny!" Bea exclaims. "But I'll smile for my picture, unlike George Washington."

"I heard he never smiled because he had wooden teeth," I say.

"He did wear false teeth," Bea replies, "but they weren't made of wood. Some of them were made from ivory, and some were *real* teeth from other people!"

"*Ew!*" Jenny and I make throw-up faces.

"I know, right?" Bea replies. "I've got the whole scoop on our first prez because I'm doing my history report on him. Did you know he was voted into office unanimously? That means everyone wanted him to be president. He had crummy teeth, but he was super popular."

"I'm doing my report on Thomas Jefferson," Jenny says. "He was popular too because he wrote the Declaration of Independence." Jenny looks at me. "Which president are you researching, Vicka?"

"I haven't decided yet," I say.

"Well, there are lots of great presidents to choose from," Bea says. "Abraham Lincoln . . . Theodore Roosevelt . . . John F. Kennedy . . ."

I nod, happy to have Bea's suggestions because they are all good choices. Every research book I checked out at the library has pages and pages packed with interesting facts and glossy photos of Lincoln, Roosevelt, and Kennedy. But I'm still looking for the perfect president for me. Someone who did great things but wasn't so flashy and famous. All I can do is keep looking.

Chapter 8

Strawberry Crush

Early on Monday morning, Sofia helps me carry three containers of chocolate-covered strawberries to school. We get there just as our custodian, Mr. Hamilton, is unlocking the main doors. "Looks like I've got a couple of early birds today!" he says to Sofia and me.

"We made chocolate-covered strawberries for my class," I reply. "Would you like one, Mr. Hamilton?"

"Don't mind if I do," Mr. Hamilton says as I open one of the containers. "Is it your birthday?"

"No," I reply. "I'm running for sixth-grade class president!"

"Vote for Vicka!" Sofia shouts. "She's the *berry* best!"

Mr. Hamilton chuckles as he takes a strawberry and reads the pendant stuck in it. Sofia had the clever idea of making toothpick pendants to stick in each berry. We worked on them all day yesterday, but it was worth it. They look super fantabulous!

Mr. Hamilton bites into the strawberry, getting red, white, and blue sprinkles in his whiskers. "Yum! Kids will eat up your campaign in no time, Victoria. What's your platform?"

"I want to plant a school garden," I reply. "We could grow strawberries and other yummy food there. We could even compost lunch scraps to make our own dirt and learn about soil and stuff."

"I do some gardening myself," Mr. Hamilton says. "Last year I built a backyard compost bin. Let me know if you need help building one for the school, President Victoria."

"Thanks, Mr. Hamilton!" I say. "But I'm not president yet."

"Then consider me the newest member of your campaign team," he replies, sticking the toothpick in the pocket of his work shirt so that the paper pendant shows.

I give Mr. Hamilton a big smile—and another strawberry!

As Mr. Hamilton walks away, keys jangling on his belt, chocolate-covered strawberry in his hand, Bea and Jenny arrive wearing the campaign buttons we made at our sleepover. Each button has a picture of Poco, begging and looking as adorable as ever.

We decided to make buttons instead of posters so people could wear a pic of my pup everywhere they go! Like Lucas said, Poco really is helping me win the election!

As Sofia heads off to start her day, Bea, Jenny, and I station ourselves near the entrance to our sixth-grade wing. When kids begin arriving for the day, we hand out chocolate-covered strawberries to everyone.

"Vote for Vicka!" Bea and Jenny shout as they pass around the treats. "She's the *berry* best!"

"Vote for me," I say, giving a strawberry to Sam. "As president, I promise to make our school a greener place by planting a garden! Our whole class can pitch in. It will be fun! We could even grow strawberries!"

"I'm *berry* sorry," Sam says, munching on the treat. "It's a good idea, but I'm voting for Henry. All of us guys are."

"Oh," I say, trying to hide my disappointment. "That's okay. I mean, everyone gets to vote for the candidate they like best. But, in my opinion, this shouldn't be about friends voting for friends. It should be about choosing the best person for the job."

"You're right," Sam says. "But I'm still voting for Henry."

"Hey, Vicka, got a strawberry for me?" I turn to see Drew looking over my shoulder.

"Oh!" I say, nearly tipping the container as I jerk around to face my crush. "Um . . . sure . . . I mean, yes! Of course! Take as many as you want!"

Sam raises his eyebrows.

Drew grins and takes a berry. "One should be plenty."

I feel my cheeks sizzle, and my glasses slide down my sweaty nose. But I don't dare bump them back up for fear I'll spill all the strawberries on Drew's sneakers, just like I did with my lunch tray. Then he'll know I'm an unfortunate klutz! "Oh . . . um . . . by the way," I say, stumbling over my campaign pitch. "Vote for me! Please? I will make a very . . . I mean a *berry* good president." My glasses slip down another notch. *¡Uf!*

"I'd like to vote for you," Drew says. "But I'm on Henry's team in this election."

"See?" Sam says to me. "Told ya us guys are sticking together."

"But Henry is only running for president because you dared him to do it," I tell Drew, finding my voice and my courage again.

"True that," Drew replies. "But I *had* to dare him. It was the only way I could get him to run. I really do think Henry will make a great class prez. He acts like a total clown because he doesn't think anyone will take him seriously. But he's got good ideas. If he gets voted into office, it could give him the boost he needs to go after more than just a few laughs."

Sam nods. "Henry's a good egg. A bit scrambled, but good."

I have to admit I've never thought of Henry as anything other than a big goofball. But then I don't know him as well as Drew and Sam do. They must see something in him that I've never taken the time to notice before.

Drew sticks the paper pendant from his strawberry in the rim of his baseball cap. "Good luck, Vicka!" he says. "May the best candidate win!"

"Yeah, good luck," Sam adds, tucking his pendant behind the bow of his glasses. As he and Drew walk off, I can't help but smile. My crush is wearing my name on his cap! And even if he and Sam don't vote for me, maybe some of the other guys will see them wearing my pendant and give my campaign a little more thought.

Just then, Annelise arrives, carrying a big box of candy bars that are plastered with stickers of her face. She freezes when she sees me.

"What do you think you're doing?" she asks.

"I'm campaigning," I reply, holding a strawberry out to her. "Vote for me! I will make our school the *berry* best!"

Annelise scowls. She doesn't take the strawberry, even though I know she loves them. I've seen her slurping strawberry smoothies in the mall's food court lots of times. "How do you plan to do that?" she asks.

"By getting everyone to pitch in and plant a school garden so we can grow good stuff to eat, like strawberries!"

Annelise gives me a blank stare. Then she bursts out laughing. "A dirty garden? Filled with worms and bugs? *That's* your great plan for our school?" She laughs even louder, and kids are starting to look at us. "And to think I was worried you would split the girls' vote. I'm not worried now!"

Annelise prances away with her candy bars, but as she looks around at all the kids eating strawberries and waving my cute toothpick pendants, I see a stormy shadow cross her face.

When the bell rings a few minutes later, Bea and Jenny rejoin me. "We sold out!" Bea says as they hand me their empty containers. "Everyone loved the berries. And lots of kids listened when we told them about your plan for a school garden. I think they really like the idea!"

Jenny nods excitedly, then shoots a look down the hallway at Annelise. She's dodging back and forth between kids, shoving candy bars into their hands. "Everyone except Annelise, that is. When she saw Katie and Grace taking strawberries from me, she made them throw the berries away! Then she told them to keep away from the *enemy.*"

I gulp.

"She still thinks I'm her enemy? I was hoping she'd forgotten. Remember how, in second grade, she put a spider in Henry's sandwich after he chased her with one at recess? He almost ate it! And last year, she put a frog in Felicia's backpack after Felicia told on her for cheating on a math quiz." I look nervously at Annelise. "She's got worms and bugs on her mind, now that she knows about my garden plans. I wonder what she'll do to *me*."

"Those were just dumb kid pranks," Jenny says. "We're in middle school now. I'm sure Annelise has matured."

I nod because I want to believe Jenny, but I bite my lip because I don't.

Chapter 9

Speech Day

Halfway through the week, I start to think Jenny was right after all. I haven't found any creepy crawlies in my lunch or backpack. Maybe Annelise really has given up on childish pranks. Either that or she's been too busy working on her campaign to plot her revenge against me. That's one good thing about being unfortunately average. People forget you're around!

Today is the day we have to give our stump speeches. I'm nervous about speaking in front of a whole lunchroom of classmates, but I'm excited too because the Caf will be the perfect place to tell everyone about my compost plans! I even found an old brown banana at the bottom of our fruit bowl at breakfast this morning. It must have been there for a long time because it's way too bruised and squishy to eat. But it's perfect for putting into my compost bucket! Mr. Hamilton let me borrow an extra pail he keeps in his supply closet.

I took it home last night and used Mom's sparkly washi tape to spell COMPOST across it. Then I looked through her scrapbooking stickers and jazzed up the bucket with tie-dye flowers, neon fruit, and cartoon vegetables! Composting may be a little yucky, but it doesn't have to be boring. We can make it colorful and fun. When everyone sees me put my rotten banana into a funky compost bucket, my speech will shine!

Annelise has been practicing her speech with Katie and Grace all week. Henry, on the other hand, doesn't seem to care about his speech at all. Yesterday Drew asked him if he was ready to give it and Henry replied, "Dude, is that tomorrow?"

I am somewhere in the middle with my speech. Sofia helped me write it, and I practiced it a few times with Bea and Jenny. Last night, I tried practicing in front of Poco too, but he fell asleep as soon as I started. ¡Ay! Let's hope my classmates can stay awake longer than my Chihuahua!

"I have something for you," Bea tells me when we get to the lunchroom later. Mrs. Larson tracked us down earlier and gave us passes so we could grab lunch before it's time to give my speech, but I'm too nervous to eat.

"What is it?" I ask as Bea reaches into her pocket.

"Think of it as a good luck charm," she says, then drops a small, smooth stone into my hand. The word *Confidence* is written on it in bold, sparkly letters.

"Hide it in your hand while you speak," Bea explains. "It will remind you that you've already got what it takes to shine!"

I give the rock a squeeze. Then I give Bea a hug! Mom was right. The first thing every candidate needs is the support of her family and friends. With Sofia, Bea, and Jenny on my side, I feel like I can really *rock* this election!

"Testing . . . testing . . . one . . . two . . . three . . ." Mrs. Larson taps a microphone she's setting up at the far end of the Caf as Mr. Hamilton adjusts the volume on a speaker. He gives her the thumbs-up when the sound is right, then places an upside-down milk crate behind the mic stand and three chairs nearby for Annelise, Henry, and me.

Principal Oates arrives and starts chatting with some of the teachers. All my classmates are here now, huddled up at tables, eating today's hot lunch: tacos, curly fries, baby carrots, and brownies. It's one of my favorite meals, but, like I said, my stomach is doing a gymnastics routine today. I give my confidence rock another squeeze to settle my *stomach*saults.

Just then, Annelise walks in with her nose in her phone. She's wearing a pink satin sash across her sparkly campaign T-shirt. The sash sparkles too. As

Annelise breezes past us, Bea and I read the glittery words printed on her sash: *Future President.*

Then we look at each other and do throw-up faces.

When Jenny gets to the lunchroom a minute later, I leave her and Bea with the funky compost bucket and walk over to where Annelise is sitting by the microphone. She glances up from her screen and gives my outfit the once-over as I sit down next to her. "*That's* what you're wearing?" she asks.

I frown and look myself over too. Blue cami, orange hoodie, faded jeans, lime green sneakers. It's the kind of outfit I always wear. "What's wrong with what I'm wearing?" I ask, looking at Annelise again.

"It's just so *ordinary*," she replies, straightening her sash. "If you end up being my vice president, you're going to have to get some new outfits."

Annelise goes back to thumbing her screen.

I scoot down a chair.

"Sixth-grade students, may I have your attention, please?" Mrs. Larson's voice booms from the microphone speaker. Quickly, Mr. Hamilton adjusts the volume. Everyone looks up from their tacos. "Please chew quietly and refrain from chatting as your three presidential candidates present their stump speeches for your enjoyment and consideration!"

A loud crash makes everyone turn and look toward the far end of the Caf. Henry has just galloped in and ran right into one of the big trash cans that sits near the doorway! Fortunately, he doesn't knock it over because the can is filled to the top with lunchroom garbage.

"Did I miss anything?" Henry asks, chugging up to us, out of breath. He plops down in the empty chair between Annelise and me, sweat glistening on his forehead. Wiping his face with the sleeve of his wrestling sweatshirt, he adds, "I was lifting weights and lost track of time. Sorry to keep you waiting."

"*I'm* sorry you showed up," Annelise says, fanning her wrinkled nose. "Seriously, Henry, you smell worse than a skunk!"

"*Awww* . . . thank you, my little stinker," Henry replies in a lovey-dovey voice. He starts to lean in for a hug.

Annelise shrieks and shoves him away.

I snicker and fan my nose too because, seriously? He really does smell bad!

"First up . . . Annelise Cooper!" Mrs. Larson announces.

"Gladly," Annelise says, tucking away her phone. She flits over to the microphone and steps up onto the milk crate. It wobbles a little, but she plants her feet firmly and straightens her sash. "I don't have to tell you who I am," she says into the microphone, "but I will anyway. I am Annelise Cooper. Your. NEXT. **PRESIDENT!**" She finds Katie and Grace in the crowd and gives them a quick nod.

Katie and Grace jump up and shoot off party poppers. A burst of sparkly confetti and colorful streamers shower down around us. Annelise smiles approvingly. "As you can see, I will add lots of *sparkle* and *fun* to our class. My number-one goal is to make our school a stink-free zone!"

Katie and Grace grab cans of air freshener and start spraying them all around the room. Soon kids are protecting their tacos from the lilac-scented cloud that's settling on their lunch trays.

"With my PEE-YOO! policy in place, every locker will have an air freshener and every student a bottle of body spray!" Annelise glares at Henry. "No student will stink when I'm in charge!"

Henry scratches his armpit.

Katie and Grace cheer wildly. Annelise curtsies, then pulls out her phone, turns around, and snaps a selfie with all of us in the background.

"Betchya she splashes that picture all over the Web before the next bell rings," Henry says to me out of the corner of his mouth.

I nod in agreement as Annelise hops down from the milk crate, returns to her chair, and starts editing the picture.

"Next we will hear from Henry Humphrey!" Mrs. Larson announces.

"Good luck," I whisper to Henry.

"Thanks. I'll need it," he whispers back.

As Henry saunters up to the microphone, all the boys whoop and holler. Lots of girls join in too. Principal Oates and Mrs. Larson step forward, shushing everyone as Henry teeters on the milk crate like a boulder on the edge of a cliff. He hunches over the microphone and says, "What kid likes Mondays? No kid, that's who. With me as class president, you can say goodbye to *Mon*days forever."

Everyone shoots puzzled looks around the room.

"You heard me right," Henry continues. "Goodbye, *Mon*day. Hello, *Mud*day! As president, I will devote the first day of every week to the study of *mud*. I'm talking about mud wrestling in P.E. Mud sculptures in art. Mud volcanoes in science. *Mud Through the Ages* in history. And for lunch? Chocolate mud pie, of course!"

I glance at the lunch ladies who are gathered by the kitchen doorway, listening. They whisper something to each other, laugh, and then shake their heads. Principal Oates rolls her eyes.

But all the kids start cheering. Henry grins from ear to sweaty ear. Then he punches the air and shouts, "Mud!"

Henry's buddies start pounding their fists on the tables, chanting, "Mud! Mud! Mud!"

Everyone joins in. Except Annelise. She's too busy posting pictures of herself. I don't chant either because Mrs. Larson has just given me the signal.

It's *my* turn to speak.

Gulp!

Chapter 10

Ishy, Squishy

Squeezing my confidence rock, I gather up my courage and walk over to the milk crate. Henry gives me a high five as he lumbers down. I step up, my knees turning to jelly. The crate wobbles. I grab the microphone stand to steady myself. Unfortunately, the microphone gets knocked crooked when I do. It screeches like an alley cat.

SCREECH!!!

Everyone drops their tacos and clamps their hands over their ears, crying out in pain. Mr. Hamilton rushes over to the speaker and starts turning knobs until the screeching stops. *¡Uf!*

"Oops . . . sorry about that," I say into the mic, which is now pointing at my nose instead of my mouth. But I don't dare touch it again, so I teeter on my tiptoes and keep on going. "Um . . . as class president, my first promise is to never touch a microphone again."

A few kids unclamp their ears, laughing at my comment. Soon everyone is settling down, munching tacos again, and listening to me. *Whew!* I messed up, but they're giving me a second chance.

I glance toward the dish room and see Bea and Jenny, sending me a big dose of smiles. I take a deep breath and start again. "My name is Victoria Torres, and I plan to change the way we do lunch."

Sam perks up. "Cool! Are you gonna get vending machines? That would be sick! I vote for heat-n-eat burritos. Those things are so disgusting, they're good!"

A bunch of Sam's buddies murmur in agreement. Henry turns around in his chair and starts discussing the finer points of the heat-n-eat burrito with Drew.

Annelise glances up from her phone and makes a disgusted face.

"Um . . . sorry, no vending machines," I say, then quickly add, "but, like Henry, I will give you *dirt*. Not just on the first day of the week, but *every* day!"

The boys stop talking and start listening again. Drew raises his eyebrows at me curiously.

"And, like Annelise," I continue, looking away from Drew to keep my heart from having a crush attack, "I promise there will be some new smells around here. They won't always be pleasant, but some of them will be delicious!"

Annelise gives me the stink eye, but some of the teachers and lunch ladies stop chatting with each other and look at me, waiting to hear more. I risk another glance at Drew. He raises his eyebrows higher. I forge ahead like George Washington crossing the Potomac River.

"As class president, I will make our school a greener place," I say. "My plan is to plant a garden in our school's courtyard. We can even make our own compost!"

"What's *compost*?" someone calls out.

"It's what we'll get when we mix our lunchroom food scraps with grass clippings and leaves," I explain. "All that organic stuff decays into compost, which will make our garden dirt really good for growing plants."

Henry gives me a wide grin, then fist pumps the air. "Dirt!" he shouts.

Drew raises his fist too. So does Sam. "Dirt!" they shout together. "Wasting stuff is easy," I say, feeling more confident. "Dumping our lunch trays into a trash can takes no time at all. Separating out the paper and plastic from the apple cores and orange peelings will take more time, but not everything we do has to be quick and easy. Changing our habits will change our school in a good way."

I pause, looking over the sea of faces filling the crowded room. Everyone is listening to me. Then, much to my surprise, I see Sofia standing way in back! She smiles and give me a nod. My sister is here, supporting me! She may drive me crazy sometimes, but today I'm so happy to have her on my side.

I take a deep breath and squeeze my rock tighter. "If we save our lunch scraps in a bucket every day, we can add them to a compost bin outside. While we study algebra and write compositions and dissect frog brains, all those yucky food scraps will be turning into something sweet—dirt! Which we can use to grow more food!"

I reach into my hoodie pocket and pull out the ishy-squishy brown banana I tucked there before my speech. I hold it up for everyone to see.

"*Ewww!*" Annelise says, wrinkling her nose at my banana. "Disgusting!" She points her phone at me. *Click!*

"It *is* disgusting," I say. "Not to mention stinky." I sniff the banana and make a face.

Everyone laughs.

I hear another *Click!*

"But this banana is about to change our school!" Hopping down from the milk crate, I walk past Henry, certain he is going to do something goofy like grab the banana and act like a monkey. Instead, he looks at me with raised eyebrows and a curious grin, like he is really interested in hearing more about my plan.

Walking over to Bea, I drop the banana into the colorful compost bucket she's holding. Jenny quickly starts scraping a tray heaped with orange peelings, apple cores, and a half-eaten taco into the bucket too.

Annelise jumps to her feet. "You want us to save our *garbage*? That's *gross*."

"It's not gross," Henry tells Annelise. "It's *green*."

I give Henry a smile. "Composting our food scraps is good for the environment," I continue. "It's good for our school too, because all that compost will turn into dirt that we can use to grow beautiful gardens!"

Kids start whispering to each other. Some of the teachers nod and smile at me. So do the lunch ladies.

Mrs. Larson gives me a thumbs up. Mr. Hamilton even salutes!

Principal Oates steps forward. "Thank you, Victoria, for sharing your very interesting idea with us. While all the candidates did a fine job, I think I speak for the teachers and staff when I say your platform has the most a-*peel*."

Everyone applauds our principal's joke.

Annelise gives me a death stare.

As the bell rings for afternoon classes, the Caf begins to clear. Even though we don't have a compost bin yet, some kids carry their trays to Bea and scrape them into the funky bucket anyway! I feel like the most *above*-average girl in the world!

Chapter 11

Vicka Stinks!

After giving my stump speech, the rest of the week flies by. With Election Day right around the corner, all the hallways at Middleton Middle School are bright with candidate posters and fliers. This morning, Bea brings a new batch of posters to school. Each one has a super cute honeybee, holding a calculator.

"I'll help you hang them up!" I tell my BFF.

When Jenny arrives a minute later, she goes crazy for the cute posters too. "I can't wait to vote for both of you!" she says. "Let's hang some in the Caf. Then everyone will see them."

"Good idea," I reply.

"Roger that," Bea adds.

"But as we head down the hall toward the lunchroom, we can't get through because a crowd of kids is blocking the way. I catch a glimpse of Annelise in the middle of the mob, handing out something to everyone.

"Annelise must have brought some new swag to school," I say. "I wonder what it is this time . . . perfume? Shower gel? Flavored lip gloss?"

"I don't know," Bea says, standing on her tiptoes, trying to see past everyone. "But whatever it is, lots of kids want it!"

"Don't shove!" we hear Annelise shout. "I have plenty of stickers for everyone! Be sure to share them with all your friends!"

Jenny, Bea, and I make puzzled faces at each other. "Stickers?" I say. "That's what everyone is going gaga over?"

Jenny shrugs. "Maybe they're sealed in gold?"

I snicker at her joke. "Limited edition," I add.

We both laugh, then turn to Bea, but she isn't laughing along with us. In fact, she's frowning, her eyes glued to the kids who are walking away from the mob with stickers stuck to their shirts.

"What's the matter, Bea?" I ask, trying to catch a glimpse of the stickers. "Is it another annoying selfie of Annelise?"

Bea shakes her head grimly. "No, it's not Annelise. It's *you*."

I blink with surprise. "Me?! But that's crazy! Annelise would never put *my* picture on her stickers. I'm the enemy!"

Just then, Henry steps out from the crowd, sees us, and saunters over. My eyes go buggy when I get a good look at the sticker on his chest. Bea was right!

My picture is on it! But my face is tinted *green*. The banana I'm smelling is *brown*. Annelise must have snapped an awful photo of me while I was giving my stump speech!

But the thing that really makes my heart shrivel to the size of a raisin is the slogan that's stamped across my picture. *Vicka Stinks!*

"Check it out, Vicka," Henry says as he rubs his fingernail across the sticker. "It's scratch-n-sniff! Go ahead, take a whiff."

Cautiously, I lean in to sniff the sticker. Then I step back quickly and cover my nose. The sticker smells like rotten eggs!

Henry snickers when he sees the shocked look on my face. He waves his hand in front of his nose and jokes, "Pee-yoo, Vicka! You stink as bad as me!" Then he walks away, chuckling to himself.

Jenny and Bea glare at Annelise who is still happily handing out stinky stickers to all of our classmates. I even see some seventh and eighth graders taking them!

"This means *war*," Jenny says through gritted teeth.

Bea nods sharply. "I say we take a few pictures of *her*."

"*Oooh . . .* " Jenny says, rubbing her hands together like a mad scientist. "Annelise sits across from me in study hall. She's always picking her nose when she thinks no one is looking. I'll have my phone camera charged up and ready to go."

Bea's eyes dance like she's morphing into an evil elf. "I've got the perfect slogan to go with that picture . . . 'Annelise for president . . . *s*not!'"

"Good one!" Jenny says, giving Bea a high five. "And check out that zit on her chin. It looks like a volcano, ready to erupt. I'll get a close-up and add the caption: 'Run for your lives!'"

My jaw drops as my BFFs laugh hysterically. "What's happening to you two?" I ask. "Five minutes ago you were into cute bumblebee posters. Now you want to slam Annelise with boogers and zits?"

Bea stops laughing and gives me a surprised look. "Those stinky stickers are super mean, Vicka! Annelise deserves a taste of her own medicine."

Jenny nods in agreement. "She needs to be taken down a few notches."

My friends are right. Annelise thinks way too much of herself. Fighting back with a few rotten pictures of her might teach her a lesson. But, on the other hand, if I agree to their plan, am I any better than Annelise?

"I don't like the stickers either," I finally say, "but I don't want to stoop to her level."

Just then, a bunch of kids break away from the crowd, giving us a clear view of Annelise. Her shirt is dotted with so many stinky stickers it looks like she has a bad case of Vicka pox.

Jenny steps toward Annelise and points an accusing finger at her shirt. "Seriously?" she hisses. "Stinky stickers? How could you be so mean?"

Annelise purses her lips and tosses back her long, shiny hair. "Don't have a spaz," she tells Jenny. "My dad says the only way to win an election is to throw a little mud. I'm just being a good politician."

"What about being a good *friend*?" Bea snarls. "I'd rather lose the election and keep my friends than win it and make enemies!"

Annelise smirks. "Cute," she says. "You should put that on a T-shirt."

I'm steaming mad, but I keep quiet. If I start playing the insult game, I know I'll lose my cool and fight fire with fire. Then Annelise wins.

Jenny's eyes burn holes in the back of Annelise's head as she marches away. "Just *one* crummy picture of her, Vicka. *Pleeease?* She totally deserves it!"

"*No* ugly photos of Annelise," I say firmly. I look back and forth between my BFFs. "Promise?"

Jenny and Bea sigh. "Promise," they grumble reluctantly.

"Let's go, then," I say. "We'll have to put up Bea's posters later or we'll be late for class."

I hold my head high as we walk down the hallway together, even though my stinky green face keeps popping up on T-shirts and backpacks and locker doors.

I hurry from classroom to classroom all morning, eyes low, but I still catch glimpses of those awful stickers. When I get to Mrs. Larson's classroom after lunch, there's even one stuck to my desk! Quickly, I cover it with my history book. Then I sit down and close my eyes tight, tighter, tightest. It makes me feel like I'm invisible, which, for once, I wish I were. It also helps me keep the tears that are trying to escape, locked inside me.

Chapter 12

Sweet Smells and LOLs

Unfortunately, I can't keep my eyes shut all afternoon. By the time the final bell rings, I see stinky stickers dotting every hallway at Middleton Middle School. Almost every kid I rush past on my way out the door is wearing a pea green picture of me holding a rotten banana. Some of the kids point at me and say, "Hey, isn't that the girl who's running for president? *Ick*toria Torres?" Then they laugh like I'm one big joke.

I still want to be class president, but is it worth staying in the race if it means being called *Icka* for the rest of the campaign? For the rest of the year?? Maybe for the rest of my unfortunately average life???

Even if I do get elected president, it doesn't mean kids will actually scrape their trays into a bucket. Annelise and her friends won't, that's for sure. Henry and his buddies will probably use the compost for food fights, which will make the lunch ladies angry. Then they will blame me for the mess! It's easy to make a big promise but harder to turn it into something that actually shines.

I'm so upset about the stickers, I don't even wait for Bea to catch up with me on my way home from school. Instead, I run the whole way to my house, tears streaming down my cheeks. When I finally get inside, I slam the front door behind me, drop my backpack, and practically trample Lucas as I run upstairs. I don't even stop to apologize for flattening him against the stair rail or to answer Abuela when I hear her voice calling after me. My grandmother must be here to babysit Lucas again.

Ducking into my bedroom, I toss my glasses onto my nightstand, fall onto my bed, and let all the tears

I've been holding inside gush out of me. I hear Poco whimpering at the foot of my bed. A moment later, I feel his soft, warm tongue licking away my tears. I pull him in and hug him tight.

"I don't want to stand out in a crowd if it means getting laughed at," I tell my pup. "But I don't want to settle for blending in either. I want to shine! Not in a glittery way, like Annelise. And not as a total clown, like Henry. Still, it seems like that's what my classmates want. Can that really be all that matters to sixth graders? Sweet smells and LOLs?"

There's a knock on my bedroom door. Poco hops up and wags his tail as Abuela peeks in.

I sit up and rub tears from my eyes. "Hi, Abuela."

"Hello, Victoria," Abuela replies. "May I come in?"

"*Sí*," I say, making room for her to sit down next to me. "I'm sorry I ignored you earlier. I didn't want to talk to anyone right then."

"Lucas told me you were crying. I thought he must be mistaken, but now I see that it's true." She pats my knee. Poco curls up next to us. "Would you like to talk now?"

Sometimes it's annoying when my family wants to know everything that's going on in my life. But other times, like today, all I want is for someone to make everything better.

Abuela listens quietly as I start from the beginning. I tell her how much everyone loved the chocolate-covered strawberries I brought to school and how Mr. Hamilton thinks my idea for a compost bin is so good he has already volunteered to build it.

"Some of my classmates told me they like the idea too, and I was beginning to believe I really could get elected president. But then, today, Annelise brought stickers to school—ugly *green* stickers with *my* picture! When you scratch them they smell worse than Oscar the Grouch's garbage can! Now my stinky face is stuck all over the school, and everyone is laughing at me. Jenny and Bea think I should get back at Annelise for being so mean. They want to take ugly pictures of her and spread them around school too."

Abuela takes a deep breath and lets it out slowly. "What do you think of that idea?" she asks.

"I'm super angry with Annelise, but I don't want to be like her," I reply. "Besides, everyone would say I was being totally unoriginal. Then they'd call me a stinky *copycat*."

Abuela nods. "I'm happy to hear that you don't want to run a negative campaign, Victoria. And I'm proud of you for standing up to your friends. Winning at all costs comes with a price. In the end, this is *your* campaign. One election isn't worth giving up what you stand for. Be the candidate you want to be, not the one people tell you to be."

I sigh. "I thought running for president would make me sparkle and shine. Instead, it's made me green and stinky. I don't know what I was thinking. I never thought I'd say it, but I wish I could go back to being plain, old, average me. "

"There's nothing wrong with being plain, old, average you," Abuela says. "Some of our greatest leaders started out that way. Abraham Lincoln is one example. He had the most ordinary childhood you can imagine. Most of what he learned, he taught himself. He put up with a lot of mean comments and angry opponents along the way, but he went on to be our country's greatest president. And don't forget about Guadalupe Victoria."

"Who's she?" I ask.

"*He* was the first president of Mexico. Guadalupe was his first name and Victoria, his last," Abuela explains as she scratches my back. "Victoria faced many, many problems as president. There were people who thought of him as their enemy and tried to take away his power. I'm sure he doubted himself at times, but he didn't give up. And as a result, he brought great change to Mexico. He ended slavery there, promoted education, and established a national treasury."

"He did all that?" I ask.

Abuela nods. "A president must work hard for all the people, even if some of them don't show their appreciation. If you are serious about making a difference at school, your classmates will sense that, despite the stinky stickers. Be yourself, Victoria, stick to what matters, and see how you shine!"

"But, Abuela, what if I don't win?" I ask.

"Then you congratulate the winner and walk away from the election holding your head high because you worked your hardest and didn't trample anyone along the way."

"Except for Lucas," I say, cringing. "I trampled him a minute ago. I should go tell him I'm sorry."

Abuela smiles and gives me a hug. "Stay true to who you are, Victoria Torres. Do that, and you can't lose."

Chapter 13

New Rules

All weekend I stay out of sight and work on my president report for Mrs. Larson's class. I decide to write about President Victoria, hoping that Mrs. Larson won't mind that I chose a president from another country. I find information about him online. Abuela gives me some books that have more info about him. Some of them are written in Spanish, so she helps me translate the parts I don't understand. I'm still upset about what happened last week at school, but working on my report gives me something else to think about. Plus, reading about President Victoria is really interesting. He isn't as well known as

George Washington, but they were both the first president of their countries. And, like Abraham Lincoln, he did great things despite the meanies who tried to diss him. Plus, President Victoria has the coolest name of all the presidents, don't you think?

In history class on Monday, Principal Oates's voice comes over the intercom. "With class elections in the final stretch, it has come to my attention that some last-minute campaign rules are needed. Beginning immediately, no one may use stickers for promoting their favorite candidate unless they plan to scrape them off walls and lockers after school. Mr. Hamilton spent the entire morning doing just that, so I know he is not a fan of the job."

Everyone shoots looks at Annelise. Her jaw twitches, and her cheeks brighten.

"The point of our school's campaign is to raise up leaders who will inspire and motivate our student body to make positive changes for the benefit of our whole school," Principal Oates continues. "No one should be made to feel unworthy of that endeavor. Therefore, negative photos and slogans are hereby strictly forbidden. Any candidate who breaks this rule, inside or outside of our school building, will have their names removed from the election roster. In short, every candidate will run a clean campaign from now on. Thank you, students, for your cooperation in this matter."

Sam raises his hand after the intercom clicks off. "But what about Henry? He can't run a clean campaign. It's all about mud!"

"I think what Principal Oates is getting at is negative campaigning," Mrs. Larson says. "When a candidate is desperate to win, he or she sometimes resorts to making rude and far-fetched statements about his or her opponent."

Annelise shifts in her chair, like a colony of fire ants are camping in her underwear. "My father says politics isn't for wimps. If you don't have thick skin, you shouldn't run for office."

"Oh, yeah?" Drew says, turning sharply toward Annelise. "My *mom* says politicians who bash their opponents are bullies and cowards. When I showed her one of *your* smelly stickers, she said that kind of campaigning is a stupid waste of time."

Annelise starts squirming again. "Vicka is the one who brought a rotten banana to school," she blurts. "It's not my fault if she decided to wave it around in front of my camera."

"I was trying to make a point about what really matters at our school," I interrupt. "There are more important things to talk about than whether or not we smell like gym socks."

Henry snorts a laugh, then starts applauding, along with Drew. As everyone joins in, Annelise's cheeks start to look like they could stop traffic.

At the end of class, Mrs. Larson reminds us to leave our president reports in the homework basket on her desk. "After I grade them, I'll display the reports as part of our Election Day festivities," she explains. "Oh, that reminds me, Principal Oates caught me before class to say that all candidates should meet in the school auditorium during seventh period. A member of the student council will photograph you for the school's newsletter and website."

"Today?!" Annelise shrieks. "But I didn't bring my sash to school! And my hair is a wreck!" She smooths back her perfectly smooth hair.

"Yes, Annelise, today," Mrs. Larson repeats.

Annelise throws her report onto Mrs. Larson's desk, then rushes out the door, phone jammed to her ear. "Hello, Mother? I need my sash *now!* Duh, yes, the pink one. Hurry!"

I wait until my classmates turn in their reports and and wander into the hallway. Then I carry my report up to Mrs. Larson's desk.

"Mine is a little different," I tell my teacher. "Everyone else wrote reports about one of our American presidents. But I researched a president from Mexico. I hope that's okay."

Mrs. Larson raises her eyebrows, intrigued. "That's more than okay, Victoria," she replies. "Which president did you write about?"

"Guadalupe Victoria," I reply. "He was Mexico's first president. He isn't famous, like Abraham Lincoln, but he ended slavery in his country too. And even though he wasn't as popular as George Washington, he didn't let his enemies get him down." I hand my report to Mrs. Larson. "If I'm class president, I want to be like him."

Mrs. Larson smiles. "I'm impressed, Victoria," she says. "And I'm proud of you for venturing outside of our nation's history to learn more about a president you admire. That required gumption and outward thinking, which are two qualities every great leader needs."

I smile even though I'm not sure what gumption means. But based on the way Mrs. Larson is skimming through my report and nodding with interest, I think gumption is a very good thing to have!

Chapter 14

Where's Annelise?

At the end of the day, Bea and I sit on the edge of the stage in our school's auditorium, filling out a survey Sofia gave us about our hopes and dreams for the school year ahead. She's going to use our answers when she writes an article about the class elections for our school newsletter and website.

I scissor kick my legs against the side of the stage and look around the dimly lit auditorium as other candidates begin to trickle in, finding places to sit while filling in their surveys. The stage isn't that far off the ground, but it feels like I'm on the edge of something new and a little bit scary. Just a few weeks ago, I was plain old ordinary me. Now I'm running for president! I don't know what this year will bring, but I'm definitely ready to find out!

The doors at the back of the auditorium open again and a tall boy I've never seen before steps inside. His hair is slicked down all neat and tidy, and his shirt is tucked into his jeans. He's even wearing a necktie— bright blue, with red and white stripes. As he takes a survey from Sofia and heads down the aisle toward us, I'm shocked when I realize it's Henry!

"Wow, Henry!" I say, as he walks up to Bea and me. "What happened to you?"

Henry shrugs and messes with the tie. "I thought I should make an effort," he replies. "Felicia loaned me a comb, and I borrowed a tie from one of Drew's nerdy friends." He lifts his arm and takes a sniff. "I even put on deodorant!"

I laugh, but Bea just sits there, staring starry-eyed at Henry. "You . . . you . . . you look nice," she finally manages to say.

Henry's ears brighten. He ducks his head and says, "Aw, shucks, Bea. Thanks."

I smile. "I guess Annelise got you to smell good after all!"

Henry chuckles, then hops up onto the stage, sitting down next to me. He starts looking over the survey questions. "Name one way you plan to make a difference at Middleton Middle School," he says, reading aloud the first question. He thinks for a moment, nods to himself, and starts writing his answer.

Peeking over his shoulder, I ask, "What are you writing?"

Henry looks up. "I've got a new idea for a big project. You inspired me, actually."

I blink with surprise as Bea looks over too. "I did?"

Henry nods. "I really dug your garden plans and what you said during your stump speech. How we really can make a difference here, even if we're only a bunch of sixth graders. It made me want to make a difference too. But now I'm thinking we could kick it up a notch and build a garden for the whole town! There's an empty lot near my house. It's overgrown with weeds and scraggly bushes. Our class could clean it up and turn it into garden plots. People could rent them out and grow their own veggies. We wouldn't charge them much, but the rent money could help us keep the lot spruced up and looking good."

As Henry goes back to his survey, I turn to Bea. We are both wide-eyed with surprise. Henry is always joking around. But today, he isn't joking at all! He seems really excited about his big idea. And I, Victoria Torres, helped him think of it! Helping people make a difference makes me feel very above average!

Just then, Sofia marches onto the stage with a camera strapped around her neck. "Looks like my sister is in charge of taking our picture too," I say as she starts ordering all of us to finish our surveys and gather on the stage. "Take it from me and don't joke around, Henry. No goofy faces, no rabbit ears, no fake farts. Sofia is all business."

Henry looks at my sister, a mischievous twinkle in his eye. "Don't worry," he says, "I'll be good."

"We'll begin with the sixth-grade candidates," Sofia announces, looking at a list of names on the clipboard she's carrying. "Bea, Grace, Henry, Victoria, and Annelise. Line up, please."

"Your wish is my command, Madame Photographer," Henry says, bowing like a genie before my sister. Sofia rolls her eyes. "You stand in back, Henry. *No* rabbit ears. I'm warning you!"

Henry bows again and then hops like a bunny to the center of the stage.

"But Annelise isn't here yet," I tell Sofia, looking around the auditorium.

Sofia, already annoyed by Henry's Easter Bunny imitation, shoots a look around. "Where is she?"

I shrug. "Beats me, but she will be super mad if we take a picture without her."

Sofia groans impatiently. "Fine, we'll start with the eighth-grade candidates and work our way down.

But she better be here by the time I get to your class, or I'll list her as absent in the photo credits."

Just then Grace's phone jingles in her pocket. She pulls it out, reads the screen, then gasps and reads it again. "Oh, no! Gosh! Oh, dear!" she cries. "Um . . . I know where she is . . . Annelise, I mean. Gotta go!"

Grace zooms out of the auditorium.

I look at Bea and Henry as we head off to wait in the wings. "What was that all about?"

Henry shrugs. "Maybe Annelise got lost in a cloud of perfume," he offers.

Henry is joking, but Bea looks worried. "It must be something more serious than that," she says. "Grace looked scared. And nothing could keep Annelise from being here other than a tragedy."

Sofia has just finished with the eighth graders and is about to move on to the seventh-grade candidates when the auditorium doors slam open. Annelise storms in. Her face is as red as dragon fire. Her hair is a frizzy mess. The satin sash she's wearing is wound around her neck like a crumpled scarf. She makes a beeline for the stage, Grace scurrying along behind her. "Which one of you losers did it?!" she snarls at Henry and me.

Henry and I exchange a puzzled look. Then we turn back to Annelise. "Did what?" I ask.

Annelise crosses her arms. "Don't play dumb with me, Victoria Torres. I know one of you locked me in the janitor's closet!"

Henry blinks with surprise. "Someone locked you in a closet? Dude, I regret to say it wasn't me."

"That's true," Grace puts in. "I saw both of them here before I got your text."

Bea pats Annelise's arm. "Tell us what happened."

Annelise shakes off Bea's hand, then starts to tell her story. "There I was, minding my own business, like always, when *BAM!* Someone plowed into me on my way to the girls' bathroom. I practically got knocked off my brand-new wedges! Before I knew what was happening, I got shoved into Mr. Hamilton's stinky supply closet. The door slammed shut! There I stood, in complete and utter darkness!"

"Oh my gosh!" Bea says. "What did you do?"

"What do you think?" Annelise snaps. "I freaked. Then I started beating on the door, threatening to murder whoever did it. I could hear the little demon snickering on the other side of the door."

Annelise pauses to catch her breath and brush back her messy hair. "It was awful. I was tripping over mop buckets and knocking down brooms, trying to find a light switch. The whole place smelled like a toilet brush! Luckily, I'm very smart and realized I had my phone with me. I texted Grace, and she got Mr. Hamilton to let me out."

Annelise looks back and forth between Henry and me, working up some angry tears. "I never thought friends of mine could be so mean!"

My mouth drops open. "I didn't have anything to do with it! And if I had known someone was planning to lock you in there, I would have stopped it."

"She's telling the truth," Bea chimes in. "Vicka wouldn't even let us take pictures of that monster zit on your chin."

Annelise's eyes go wide. Her hand flies to her face.

Henry nods thoughtfully. "Remember what Mrs. Larson told us about rogue groups resorting to drastic measures in order to give their favorite candidate an unfair advantage? I bet that's what happened here."

Annelise, Bea, Grace, and I stare at Henry like he just grew a brain.

"What?" he says, puffing up his chest with pride. "I pay attention in class. Sometimes. Besides, all this politics stuff is growing on me." He grins and straightens his tie. "Who knows? Maybe I'll run for president of the whole country someday!"

"Like that could ever happen," Annelise sasses, dabbing a zit stick to her chin.

"Why couldn't it?" I say. "I bet none of Abraham Lincoln's friends thought he would grow up to be president, but he did! Anyone can be anything they want to be if they work for it."

"Thanks for the pep talk, Little Miss Sunshine," Annelise says, tucking the pimple cream away, "but none of this is helping me figure out whose arm I need to break for locking me in that stinky closet!"

"Okay, sixth-grade candidates," Sofia calls from across the stage. "You're up."

Henry grunts like a gorilla. Then he knuckle-walks over to my sister. Sofia clamps her eyes shut and mumbles something I can't hear.

Annelise straightens her presidential sash, then barges ahead of Bea, Grace, and me. I pause when something offstage catches my eye. Drew and Sam are slipping in through a side door. Sam nudges Drew, then points across the stage at Annelise, who is primping her hair and telling Sofia she will have to stand in front so everyone can see her sash.

Drew whispers something to Sam. They both snicker.

I catch Drew's eye. He gives me a casual wave, but I arch my eyebrows like accusing question marks. *Why are you two sneaking around? Do you know anything about Annelise getting locked in the janitor's closet?*

Drew lifts a shoulder and shakes his head like he doesn't understand eyebrow talk.

But I, Victoria Torres, don't believe him for a minute.

"*Now,* Vicka!" my sister shouts impatiently. I dash across the stage and stand beside Bea. By the time the photo shoot is done—it takes a while because Henry keeps giving Annelise rabbit ears—Drew and Sam are gone.

While everyone is grabbing stuff from their lockers at the end of the day, I hunt down Drew.

Normally, talking to my crush would make my skin prickle like I'm wearing a porcupine sweater, but nothing is normal today.

Drew sees me coming and tries to duck away, but I block his path and look him square in the eye. "Did you lock Annelise in Mr. Hamilton's supply closet?"

"Huh?" Drew says, his eyes flitting around like they can't find a safe place to land. "Um . . . I . . . I . . . I might have."

I squint behind my glasses. "That was a very mean thing to do! Annelise could have gotten hurt, stumbling around in the dark. What if she had knocked over some of Mr. Hamilton's cleaning supplies? Those chemicals are dangerous! And the closet is small. She could have suffocated!"

I cross my arms and feel my cheeks burn. But I'm not blushing at Drew. I'm angry with him. Annelise may be a selfish meanie most of the time, but she is still our classmate and, sometimes, a friend. When friends are treated unfairly, even not-so-great friends, you have to stick up for them.

"Chill, Vicka," Drew says. "Sam and I checked out the closet as soon as we saw Mr. Hamilton wheel his

cleaning cart out. There were just mop buckets, garbage bags, and brooms in there. All Annelise had to
do was turn the button on the knob to get out. But she
was too busy yelling at the top of her lungs to notice."
Drew chuckles to himself. "Trust me, she had plenty
of air. Besides, we were just about to let her out when
Grace showed up with Mr. Hamilton."

"Well, that's good, but it was still mean of you to
lock her in there. Why did you do it, anyway? Henry
isn't going to lose any votes to Annelise and her *PEE-
YOO!* plan."

Drew's eyes start flitting around again. He shuf-
fles his feet and says, "I didn't do it because of Henry.
I did it because of *you*." He glances at me. "I couldn't
let Annelise get away with those stinky stickers. She
deserved to spend some time in a smelly closet."

I gulp. "You did it . . . for *me*?"

Drew nods.

My skin prickles.

My cheeks blush.

It was wrong, Wrong, *WRONG!* of Drew to lock Annelise in that closet. But I can't keep from hiding a grin. When your crush is acting like your hero, it's hard not to feel happy!

Chapter 15

And the Winner Is...

The next morning, I get dressed in a white sweater, blue skirt, and red leggings. It's Election Day and I want to look as patriotic as possible! As I head downstairs, I plan to eat a quick bowl of cereal and then scoot out the door so I can vote before school starts. But sometimes things don't go the way you plan. Which isn't always a bad thing. As I reach the bottom of the stairs, the yummy scent of blueberry pancakes and crispy bacon tells me this is going to be an *un*expected kind of day!

When I walk into the kitchen a moment later, Dad looks up from flipping pancakes and gives me a smile.

"Good morning, Bonita!" he says, cheerfully. "Happy Election Day!"

"Thanks!" I reply, giving Dad a hug. "But why aren't you at the music store? You've usually gone to work by now."

"Uncle Julio said he'd cover the store this morning so I could stay home and make you a presidential breakfast!"

I take a piece of bacon from the platter on the stove, nibbling the crispy edges. "Yum!" I say. "But . . . I might not win. It doesn't seem right to eat a presidential breakfast if I end up losing the election."

"Win or lose, you've proven yourself to be a worthy candidate," Dad tells me. "So eat up! This is your day to shine, Victoria."

Dad heaps a plate with pancakes and bacon. I carry it to the dining room table. I may be an average girl, but today I have a presidential appetite!

When I get to school later, a big, sparkly sign greets me by the main doors.

I follow a parade of kids on their way to the Caf, where the election is taking place. Along the way, I pass Mrs. Larson's door. Our president reports are posted on a bulletin board outside her classroom. Next to each report is a picture of the president it tells about. I look at the print of a painted portrait of President Guadalupe Victoria that is next to my report. He looks very spiffy in his red coat, white pants, and tall black boots. He's even wearing a blue sash around his waist! I guess Annelise isn't the only one who likes to dress up for a presidential picture!

At the far end of the display is an open space for one more photograph. The space is labeled *Class President*. By the end of the day, we'll know whose picture will go there. I wonder if it will be mine.

Walking into the Caf a minute later, I head to a row of tables that are decorated with red, white, and blue bunting. Each one holds a ballot box for the sixth-, seventh-, and eighth-grade classes. Drew, Felicia, and Katie are standing behind the sixth-grade table. Drew is dressed in red, Felicia in white, and Katie in blue. Together, they make a human flag! Since they aren't running for office, Mrs. Larson put them in charge of overseeing the election for our class. When the polls close at noon, they will help tally all the votes and give the results to Principal Oates.

"Good luck, BFF!" Bea says, greeting me with a ginormous hug.

"Right back atcha, BTF!" I say, hugging Bea back.

Bea pulls away and gives me a puzzled look. "BTF?" she asks.

I nod. "Best treasurer forever!"

Bea laughs. "BTF. I like that!"

Just then, Annelise arrives. Instead of heading to the ballot box, she walks up to Bea and me. "Good luck, Vicka," she says, shaking my hand. "May the best candidate win."

"Same to you," I reply. "I still think what happened with the janitor's closet totally *stunk*! I hope you know Henry and I didn't have anything to do with it." I hesitate, wondering if I should tell Annelise about Drew's confession to me. I don't like being a tattle-tale, but maybe this is one of those times when telling the truth is more important than keeping a secret?

"I know you didn't do it," Annelise cuts in. "When Mr. Hamilton opened the closet door, I was so relieved to be free of that sewer pit, I snapped a selfie on my phone to commemorate my rescue. When I looked at the picture last night, I could see Drew and Sam watching from around the corner."

Annelise pauses, then adds, "I'm sorry I accused you. And . . . I'm extra sorry about the stinky stickers. They were my dad's idea. I tried to talk him out of it, but this was the first time he'd ever been excited about any of my school activities." Annelise ducks her eyes. "It was selfish, but I didn't want to disappoint him, so I went along with the plan." She glances up at me. "Is there any chance we can still be friends?"

I give her arm a squeeze. "Friends for sure."

Annelise smiles with relief.

"Come on, you two," Bea says, linking up with us. "The bell is about to ring and we haven't voted yet!"

Together, we go to our class's ballot box. As Drew hands ballots to each of us he says, "I guess it's no secret who you three will be voting for."

Annelise gives Drew a death squint, then reaches into her pocket and takes out her phone. "And I guess it's no secret that *you* will be carrying my books for the next *month*," she says. "As well as my lunch tray. Unless you want Principal Oates to see *this*."

Annelise clicks up a photo on her phone. It's a selfie of her very angry face, just inside the open door of Mr. Hamilton's supply closet. Drew and Sam are photo bombing in the background.

Drew's throat clicks as he takes a gulp of air. "W-would you like chocolate or white milk with your meals?" he asks Annelise.

Annelise purses her lips and tucks her phone away. "Chocolate," she snips. "Two cartons. No straw."

I laugh at the queasy look on Drew's face as Annelise marches away to fill in her ballot. Grabbing a pencil, I look over my ballot too.

First, I put a check mark next to Bea's name. I draw a smiley face too, because she will make a great class treasurer! Then I choose Grace for class secretary because, seriously, she owns more gel pens than any girl I know.

But when I look at my choices for president, I pause. Obviously, the nice thing to do would be to vote for Annelise or Henry. After all, Annelise did apologize for the stinky stickers. And Henry has some great ideas for making a difference at our school. But, like Bea said, voting is a personal decision. You are in charge of the choices you make. I think that's how it should be every day, not just on Election Day.

My pencil hovers over my name on the ballot. What Dad said this morning is still ringing in my ears. I *have* worked hard to be a good candidate. And, if elected, I will work even harder to be a good president. I put a check mark next to my name. Then I fold my ballot and smile to myself as I place it in the box. May the best candidate win.

When the intercom crackles to life during history class later that afternoon, everyone quiets down right away. Principal Oates said she would announce the election results before the end of the day. This is it! At last, I'll know if I am the new sixth-grade class president!

"We'll start with our eighth-grade winners," Principal Oates begins. Bea and I look across the room at each other as the names of the new officers for the eighth grade, and then the seventh grade, are read.

"Good luck!" I tell Bea with my eyebrows. *"You too!"* she replies with hers. Fortunately, girls are way better at eyebrow talk than boys.

"And now for our sixth-grade officers," Principal Oates says. First, she reads the names of our new class treasurer and secretary. It's no surprise: Bea and Grace have both won! I zip across the aisle to congratulate Grace, then dash over to Bea as everyone gives her pats on the back and high fives. I give my BTF the highest high five of all!

We quiet down again as Principal Oates says, "And last but not least, here are the results of the sixth-grade presidential election. This was our school's closest race this year . . ."

Bea grabs my hand and holds it tight. Jenny jumps up from her desk and takes hold of my other hand. Win or lose, I've got friends by my side!

". . . winning by just five votes, your new sixth-grade class president is . . . Henry Humphrey!"

I hear a loud *whoop!* from the back of the room where Henry sits. His buddies are tackling him, giving our new class president congratulatory noogies.

"Aw, shucks," Henry says, when they finally let him up for air.

I drop hands with Bea and Jenny so I can lead the class in a round of applause for Henry. I'm a little sad I didn't win, but I'm also really happy that Henry did! I meant it when I told him he will be a great class president!

"And now for the sixth-grade vice-presidential results," Principal Oates continues. "Coming in second place, with 22 votes, is . . . Victoria Torres!" Bea and Jenny squeal and hug me tight because girls are too mature to give each other noogies.

"Quiet, please!" Mrs. Larson says as other kids come up to congratulate me. "Principal Oates is still speaking!"

"... and in a surprising turn of events, *also* coming in second place, with 22 votes, is Annelise Cooper! Congratulations, girls. You've tied for the vice presidency. Therefore, President Henry will choose your class's new VP."

Henry's eyes go wide. "Huh? *I've* gotta choose? Can't we just draw names?"

Mrs. Larson smiles. "No, Henry. You will choose. It will be your first presidential decision, Henry. Think carefully. Will our new vice president be Vicka or Annelise?"

Henry's shoulders tighten. Beads of sweat glisten on his forehead. His knee jiggles nervously against his desk. "Um ..." he says. "Er ..."

"You can do it, Hen," Drew says, giving his best friend a pat on the back. "Who do you pick? Vicka or Annelise?"

"I ... I ..." Henry stutters, his eyes darting between Annelise and me like he's watching a ping-pong match. But then he takes a deep breath and says,

"I choose Vicka. She has some great ideas for making our school a better place and, together, we will make them happen!"

I turn to look at Annelise. Her eyes are bright with tears, but she smiles and gives me a thumbs up. "Congratulations, Vice President Vicka," she says.

I look on with a smile as everyone crowds around Henry and me, talking about their own ideas for making a difference at our school.

It looks like I'm stuck in the middle again—right between the class prez and the rest of my classmates.

But that's okay. The future looks bright when I'm surrounded by friends!

About the Author

Julie Bowe lives in Mondovi, Wisconsin, where she writes popular books for children, including *My Last Best Friend*, which won the Paterson Prize for Books for Young People and was a Barnes & Noble 2010  Summer Reading Program book. In addition to writing for kids, she loves visiting with them at schools, libraries, conferences, and book festivals throughout the year.

Glossary

commemorate (kuh-MEM-uh-rate)——to honor and remember an important person or event

decline (di-KLINE)——to refuse something, especially in a way that is polite

distribute (di-STRIB-yoot)——to give things out to a number of people

gumption (GUHMP-shuhn)——courageous or ambitious initiative

intrigue (in-TREEG)——to interest or fascinate someone

klutz (KLUHTZ)——a clumsy person

motivate (MOH-tuh-vate)——to encourage someone to do something or want to do something

motto (MAH-toh)——a short sentence that states someone's beliefs, or is used as a rule for behavior

reassure (ree-uh-SHOOR)——to make someone feel calm and confident and give the person courage

reluctant (ri-LUHK-tuhnt)——hesitant or unwilling to do something

rogue (ROHG)——a worthless or dishonest person

roster (RAH-stur)——a list of people, especially a list that shows duties or assignments

saunter (SAWN-tur)——to walk in a slow, leisurely, or casual way

terminology (tur-muh-NAH-luh-jee)——the special vocabulary of a particular field of knowledge

Time to Talk

Questions for you and your friends

1. My classmates thought of a lot of good issues for their six-word stump speeches. What were some of them? Can you think of others?

2. I had to make a few tough decisions in the book. What do you think was the hardest decision for me to make? Explain your answer.

3. Henry, Annelise, and I all ran for class president, and I think each of us has some qualities of a good leader. Make a list of the ways each of us would make a good leader.

Just for You

Writing prompts for your journal

1. Annelise is very outgoing, and she immediately declared herself a candidate for the election. I am quieter and less confident, and it took some motivating from others to get me to run for class president. Are you more like Annelise or me? Explain your answer.

2. Sofia wrote an article about the class president candidates. Pretend you are her and write an article about me and my campaign.

3. Imagine you were running for class president. What would be your platform, or the promises you would make to improve your school? Write a speech to present your plans.

Word to the Wise

Have you ever thought about running for a class office or student council? Here are some campaign dos and don'ts that I picked up during our big election.

DO run for the right reasons. Run because you want to help people and work to improve your school.

DON'T run to become more popular, to get things that only you want, or so you can boss people around.

DO make yourself shine by talking about what you can do for your school.

DON'T put your opponent down, thinking it will make you look better. It won't!

DO make signs with memorable slogans, preferably ones that are funny and true.

DON'T let your opponents find out what your slogans are until your signs are ready. I once heard about someone stealing another person's slogans! Not good!

DO reach out to everyone.

DON'T try to just get votes from the cool kids or the smart kids or all the boys or all the girls. You'll be president for all types of kids, so you should figure out how to help all of your classmates.

DO offer small treats or tokens to help people remember you. Things like stickers, pencils, and even chocolate-covered strawberries work great!

DON'T hand out lots of over-the-top gifts. You shouldn't try to buy votes!

Cooking Corner

After reading about our patriotic chocolate-covered strawberries, I bet you're dying to make your own! Luckily, they are very easy to make and if you want to do something extra, check out my Mix-It-Up tips.

FANTABULOUS CHOCOLATE-COVERED STRAWBERRIES

INGREDIENTS

1 pound of strawberries with the stems, washed and dried

6 ounces of semisweet chocolate chips

EQUIPMENT

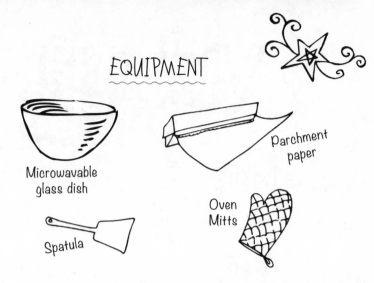

Microwavable glass dish

Parchment paper

Oven Mitts

Spatula

1. Place a sheet of parchment paper on a clean counter.

2. Pour chocolate chips into glass dish and microwave for 60 seconds. Remove and stir. (Use oven mitts if glass dish is too hot.)

3. Microwave for an additional ten seconds and stir. Repeat until all chocolate chips are melted.

4. Remove glass dish from microwave and set next to parchment paper. Holding the strawberry by the stem, dip the lower half into the chocolate and twist to completely cover the bottom half of the strawberry in chocolate.

5. Place the strawberry on the parchment paper to cool.

6. Repeat steps 4-5 with remaining strawberries.

MIX-IT-UP IDEAS

- Top the strawberries with sprinkles before the chocolate cools.

- Instead of strawberries, dip other fruits like apples into the chocolate.

- For a new flavor, try using white chocolate or butterscotch chips.

Victoria Torres

Unfortunately Average

Always looking for her way to shine!

Victoria Torres loves the family birthday party she normally has. But now that she's turning twelve, a family party seems average compared to the bash she could have with her friends at the mall's new spa store. Her mom refuses to let her have two parties and tells Victoria that's she's going to have to choose. Friends or family? Unfortunately, there's no easy answer!

When Victoria's band director asks for a volunteer to play the band's new piccolo, Victoria sees it as her shot to shine. Unfortunately, Bea wants to play piccolo too. The girls will have to audition for the spot, and the band members will select the winner. Can Victoria and Bea keep the competition friendly, or will their friendship hit a sour note?

When it comes to math, Victoria is completely average. But her sister, Sofia, is captain of the math team. When one of the team members drops out, Sofia must find a replacement—fast! Sofia volunteers Victoria and grills her in math, night and day. Can Victoria crunch enough numbers to lead the team to victory, or will her sister's bossy ways be too much to bear?

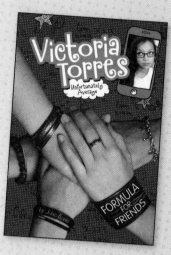

Victoria is positive being a cheerleader is the best way to secure her popularity. Her best friend, Bea, agrees to try out with her, but Victoria is going to need a lot more than Bea's support to make the squad. The competition is stiff and includes the awful Annelise. Will tryouts leave Vicka feeling far below average?

Victoria Torres dreams of being cast as Juliet in her class's production of Shakespeare's *Romeo and Juliet*. So imagine her disappointment when she's cast as Friar Laurence, a bald old man! Vicka knows that the way to shine in any role is to do your best. But another disappointed cast member is turning the class play into far more drama than even Shakespeare could have imagined!

Find out more about Victoria's unfortunately average life, plus get cool downloads and more at www.capstonekids.com

(Fortunately, it's all fun!)